# EVOKED



Celebrating
30 Years of Publishing
in India

**Other books in the series**

*A Brutal Hand*

*Insomnia*

*Body of Work*

RAVI SUBRAMANIAN

PRESENTS

# EVOKED

## THE LAVASA INCIDENT

MANSI BABBAR

HarperCollins *Publishers* India

First published in 2021

This edition published in India by HarperCollins *Publishers* in 2023
4th Floor, Tower A, Building No. 10, DLF Cyber City,
DLF Phase II, Gurugram, Haryana – 122002
www.harpercollins.co.in

2 4 6 8 10 9 7 5 3 1



P-ISBN: 978-93-5629-702-9
E-ISBN: 978-93-5629-703-6



Typeset by R. Ajith Kumar

Printed and bound at
Replika Press Pvt. Ltd.

FSC www.fsc.org MIX Paper from responsible sources FSC® C016779

This book is produced from independently certified FSC® paper to ensure responsible forest management.

# CONTENTS


| | | |
|---|---|---|
| | Prologue | 1 |
| 1. | Still Waters Run Deep | 3 |
| 2. | Writhing | 15 |
| 3. | Obsession | 24 |
| 4. | Desire | 37 |
| 5. | Trigger | 46 |
| 6. | Voices in the Head | 64 |
| 7. | Thc Puppeteer | 84 |
| 8. | Moths With Their Wings Pinned | 100 |
| 9. | Butterflies in a Jar | 120 |
| 10. | Darkest After Dawn | 137 |
| 11. | Tides Turn | 156 |
| 12. | Slender Man | 164 |
| 13. | Cacophony | 174 |
| 14. | Penitence | 192 |
| 15. | Metamorphosis | 204 |
| 16. | Evoked | 211 |
| | *Acknowledgements* | 215 |
| | *About the Author* | 217 |

## NOTE ON RAVI SUBRAMANIAN PRESENTS

For my readers who love pace, I offer *Ravi Subramanian Presents*. I've conceptualized these books as a series of short, plot-oriented, fast-paced novellas that are the book equivalent of caffeine for an exhausted mind. These are thrillers on steroids. There isn't a slow moment in these books, not a sentence that does not take the story forward, not a page that doesn't beg to be turned. Airports, railway stations, flights, buses, metros, bedrooms or even behind your laptops – you'd want to read your own copy of these books everywhere. These stories promise to hold you firmly in their grip until you reach the very end.

*Ravi Subramanian Presents* serves another purpose. I noticed that in our country, mythology and romance are popular genres and draw many capable writers. Crime writing, though, is often considered too complicated, and has not seen many writers emerge. My co-authors in this series are all brilliant writers hand-picked by me to fill this gap. Each thriller in this series is written by a talented author with a definite flair for crime writing. It has been a pleasure to work with them and to be able to provide a platform for them.

With short, fast-paced, pulse-pounding, high impact, no flab stories, *Ravi Subramanian Presents* comes with a built-in accelerator. So fasten your seatbelts and get ready for the ride!

**Ravi Subramanian**

# PROLOGUE

As the cold wind blew towards India's western coast, the hill town of Lavasa was in the grip of the worst storm it had ever witnessed. The river that cut deep into the town roared and furled its steel-grey waves. The scenic hills became a dull green backdrop as mist rose to cover them. It was twelve noon, but it felt like dusk. The sky was veiled with monsoon clouds. Distant lightning made them glow fiery red at intervals, like the slow pulse of a beast of prey.

Journalists held their mikes tight, some struggling to keep their hair from whipping into their eyes, as they reported live from the scene. Camerapersons struggled to keep their equipment steady. Standing on the bridge, one could hear the wind whistle through the gaps between the hills.

'This is the third suicide reported in Lavasa, and the second from this bridge, within three months,' a reporter pointed behind her as she spoke loudly over the mourning wind. 'The bridge you see behind me connects the two sides of Lavasa, crossing the Mutha River. This is the spot where the victims jumped to their deaths. Though there has been a lot of speculation about the victims and the possible crime scene itself, the police are yet to comment on these theories. There are also reports of a gunshot being heard by several people last evening. The police have assigned divers to recover the body of the latest victim. However, given the extreme weather conditions, the search has been put on hold. The worst of the storm has passed but for the residents of Lavasa, it's not over yet. What happened here? The whole town is eagerly awaiting an answer after a series of tragic incidents disrupted its peace—'

The reporter broke off when she spotted the chief of the Lavasa police department arrive at the bridge. He walked briskly, his men keeping the horde of reporters at bay, towards a horrified-looking man standing at the edge of the bridge.

Blood seemed to have left his face. He was staring at the bridge, silent. The senior officer called out to him.

'Inspector Suresh Mohite!'

'Yes, sir,' the inspector responded in a voice his superior barely recognized.

'Let's have a look. Take me to the spot.'

The inspector led his senior to the entrance of the bridge where some trainee officers had been posted to cordon the scene off. They saluted as the two men walked past. Usually, Mohite would return their salute. In that moment, however, he couldn't see anything but the bridge in front of him. It looked so normal and innocuous, as if nothing had happened there. His stomach turned as he approached the scene. It was still so vivid in his mind ... all of it was.

# STILL WATERS RUN DEEP

Soft sunlight spread over the enchanting hills of Lavasa, making the green landscape glimmer gold. It was an early morning in June that marked the beginning of the college year. Juniors would become seniors, and soon it would be their turn to welcome the newcomers. The monsoon had already arrived, watering the hill city with life. On the far end of the bridge that connected the two halves of Lavasa, roads twisted around the curves of hills. Hotels and residential areas were lined up neatly on this side of the town. You could see the river frolicking as it flowed east.

In one such house on a quiet road, surrounded by a beautiful garden, there was an unusual amount of activity and noise. The nameplate read 'Mohan Vyas'.

'Don't forget to take your lunchbox!' shouted a woman dressed in a cotton sari. Mrs Shilpa Mohan Vyas was in the kitchen.

'Mom, I'm in college now. School is over,' a young girl rolled her eyes as she put her sneakers on in a hurry. Her eyes sparkled with excitement, and her skin shone with vigour. She was tall and slender, with big, dark brown eyes and long hair that hung down to her waist and curled naturally at the ends. Her complexion was flawless, the colour of bright grains of wheat except for the sun-kissed pink in her cheeks. 'I am not carrying a lunch box.'

'Sevita, you can't be eating canteen food. It's not good for you, sweetheart,' Mrs Vyas argued, wiping her hands on a towel as she came out of the kitchen, and put the lunchbox in her bag. Sevita let out an exasperated sigh.

'It's cheese sandwiches,' Mrs Vyas coaxed.

'Hmm ...' Her mother did make delicious cheese sandwiches. 'Alright. Kiss me good luck.' Sevita turned her cheek towards her mother who kissed her.

'All the best, my darling. Go get your sister too. She won't open the door.' Mrs Vyas sounded a little irritated.

'C'mon, Maa. Give her some space. You know first days are hard for her,' Sevita said. She took a deep breath and went to call her sister. A corridor led to the far end of the house, where two doors faced each other. One had a beautiful ceramic nameplate that read 'Sevita' in golden letters. The door facing it was starkly devoid of any decoration. Even at eight in the morning, no light seeped from under the door.

*Of course*, Sevita thought, *she has all those thick curtains drawn again.*

'Sama?' She knocked on the door, careful not to be too loud. 'Hurry! We don't want to be late on our first day of college, do we?'

There was a soft click and the door unlocked. A girl stood there, the mirror image of Sevita. Well almost.

She had the same height and build. Her eyes were big and dark brown. Her hair was beautiful—long and curling as it reached her waist.

There was hardly any physical difference between the two girls except Sama was much paler; her skin almost seemed as if sunlight had never touched it. There was no colour at all on her face. If one looked deep enough, her eyes seemed empty.

'Ready?' Sevita asked cheerfully.

'Yes,' Sama replied in a robotic tone, although their voices would sound the same to a stranger's ears.

If it was not for the difference in their demeanour, it would be impossible to tell the twins apart.

Sevita gave her sister a big smile in spite of her coldness. Sama looked away and started walking towards the living room.

'Good morning, darling,' their father said with a wide smile. He was dressed as usual in a white kurta and pajamas. He adjusted his black-rimmed glasses and hugged Sama. 'All the best! Do well.' Sama's lips curved into a shy, lop-sided smile.

'Good morning, Mom,' she murmured to her mother. Mrs Vyas forced a smile and then looked away.

'Your lunchbox is on the table,' she said quickly and went back to cutting fruits. Sevita and her dad exchanged an exasperated look.

'Hey Sama, guess what? Starting today, we will go to college on our new scooty!' Sevita said brightly as she held up a pair of keys in front of her sister and rattled them. 'Isn't that cool?'

Sama didn't react. 'I will wait outside,' she said, picking up the lunchbox and walking out of the front door.

'Take care of her, okay?'

'Yes, dad, don't worry.' Sevita smiled, patted his round belly, and followed her sister.

Sevita kicked her new scooty to life while Sama adjusted herself on the back seat. The sisters set out for their first day at college, riding on the hillside road with edges sloping straight into the river. The sunlight was mild, and the air was clean. Sevita was thrilled by this new-found freedom. It was the start of a new phase of her life.

'This is amazing. We can have so much fun together, Sama! Let's go somewhere soon. All of us.'

Sama stared at the river flowing beside them. She remained silent. Sevita's friends were not her friends. She didn't want 'all of them' to go anywhere together.

Sevita was used to her twin's silence. This is how Sama had always been. She stayed inside her room, rarely speaking to people, and buried herself in her books or the internet. Maybe that was the reason she was so good at every subject in school. Sevita was on the other end of the spectrum, always out with her friends and talking to people. Such differences in two human beings with a 99 per cent DNA match was a case to be studied, according to their mother.

They rode through the roller-coaster-like road and across an iron bridge over the river to the other side of the town. Sevita hummed a tune while Sama watched the river. After a thirty-minute ride, they reached their college. Sevita parked the scooty and stowed away their helmets. She looked around for her friends, barely able to contain her excitement.

---

'Hi!' A shrill voice was heard from behind Sevita.

'Astha!'

A petite girl came running towards Sevita, her long ponytail swaying like a pendulum, and hugged her. 'I missed you so much. How are you?'

'I'm good. How was Pune?'

'It was awesome! The best wedding ever and—*Oh* hi, Sama,' Astha said, looking a little uncomfortable. She had just noticed Sama who was standing silently and gazing at them from a distance.

'Hi,' she said in a blank monotone.

'Well,' Astha turned to Sevita, 'They are going to the Canary Islands for their honeymoon as we speak. How cool is that!'

'Real cool, yeah.' Sevita noticed the awkwardness in the air. She was used to this too. Sama never made an effort to be a part of any social circle or activity among her peers. People knew her as the unsmiling twin.

'Astha! Sevita!' Another girl came up, almost prancing, and hugged them one by one. Shruti was tall and plump, her hair falling just an inch below her shoulders. For the next five minutes, they exchanged the details of their summer vacation and their excitement about starting college.

'—And that is when I turned him down. A guy who can't read without fumbling is so not my type. But I do want to watch that movie. Let's all plan and go.' Shruti pouted.

'Sure. What do you say, Sama?' Sevita turned to Sama, but she was gone. 'Where did she go?'

'I didn't even see her.' Shruti shook her head, puzzled.

'She was here just minutes ago. Guess she left,' Astha said, looking at Sevita.

'Listen, please make her feel comfortable. This is not easy for her. You know she can't mingle with people. At least greet her normally,' Sevita said, raising a brow at Astha.

'I am sorry, I was just shocked! It was so sudden. She was standing right there, looking like she teleported! It's ... well, I will try. Really, I will,' Astha sighed.

'That's all I'm asking you people to do, try,' Sevita said, looking at the two girls.

'But where is *he*?' Shruti asked all of a sudden, looking around.

Sevita's cheeks flushed. 'I-I don't know, haven't seen him.'

---

The girls walked across the college grounds into the building and found their classes. Sevita spotted Sama seated on a corner bench near the window. Alone. She would have liked her to join them and sit a little closer to the front rows, but she knew her sister better than that. Throughout her school days, Sama had occupied corner seats to avoid people.

There were many new faces in the class, flustered as they turned from Sevita to Sama and back again. To the familiar faces, it was no mystery, but to the others, it was the best pastime, marvelling at how different they were despite being identical twins.

'It's ridiculous when they chatter about us, thinking we can't hear them,' Sevita murmured, tired of being the favourite topic of gossip.

'I always tell you to ignore them,' someone whispered near Sevita's ear. She blushed, as goosebumps ran up and down her skin.

'Kunal!' She turned, her heart pounding. A boy in his late teens was standing behind her. His eyes were bright, his smile carefree. He was tall and had broad shoulders. Tousled hair fell on his forehead in wavy locks. Several girls in the class were already looking at him with interest.

'Hey there,' he said, his voice clear and confident. He took a seat behind Sevita who was now turning scarlet. Dressed casually in denims and a blue shirt, he radiated charm.

---

A short elderly man entered the classroom, carrying a book and a whiteboard marker. Everyone got up to greet their professor who looked much like Master Oogway in a pinstriped coat and ancient brown-framed glasses.

Far away from the others, in her corner seat, Sama didn't listen to the professor welcome them. She watched Sevita and Kunal from afar. She saw them talk in whispers when the class began, then text each other with phones hidden beneath their desks every now and then. Shruti was also texting them; she knew by observing the intervals at which they all checked their phones. Astha seemed to be paying attention to the class, but Sama saw her rolling her pen between her fingers, looking at a wall clock above the whiteboard where the professor had written the semester plan.

'Okay, so that's it about our course structure for the year and the exam patterns. You can always ask questions later. Let's introduce ourselves to everyone, shall we? I'll start. I am Professor Rawat. I have been in Lavasa my whole life, and I love gardening when I am not grading papers.'

The whole class was now abuzz, smiling and laughing.

'It always feels like a matrimonial session, I know,' Professor Rawat joked, and the class laughed. 'Okay, let's start with you folks!' He gestured at the first benchers.

Everyone stood up one by one and introduced themselves. The class was full of excited whispers.

'I am Sevita Vyas, born and brought up in Pune. We moved to Lavasa a few years ago because of my father's transfer. Umm, my hobbies are watching movies, travelling and photography.'

'What is the meaning of your name?' a guy asked, shrugging. 'I mean ... it is unique.'

'It means one who is cherished,' she said and took her seat, as some people 'oohed' from the back benches.

'Hi everyone, I am Kunal Mehta. I am from Mumbai but shifted here when my dad was transferred to Lavasa two years back. I love football, filmmaking and music.' He flashed a dazzling smile as he finished. By this time, every girl in the class had eyes only for him.

Astha introduced herself as the only daughter of a politician. She was from Lavasa. As for Shruti, both her parents were teachers. She had moved from Nagpur to Lavasa when her mother had taken up a job in the hill town, five years back. It appeared that many students had moved to Lavasa as their families shifted there for work and business.

As the introductions drew to a close, it was finally Sama's turn. She stood up noiselessly, her face blank. The whole class was staring at her. Just one glance was enough to gauge that, though identical in appearance, she was the polar opposite of Sevita.

*Worthless scum. Why should I talk to them? Why should they know me? I don't want to know them. They are useless. All of them.* The voices in her head began to hiss loudly. The professor was looking at her in surprise and confusion.

'Let us hear your name, then,' he said with a supportive smile.

'Sama Vyas. I don't have any hobbies as such. Sevita's said the rest,' Sama finished in a low voice and sat down.

'What does your name mean? Darkness?' a boy from one of the back benches taunted, making a sad clown face. Some students burst into laughter. Sevita was infuriated. Sama sat still. There was no reaction on her face, neither of anger nor of hurt. Her eyes were devoid of emotion, looking straight ahead at a wall.

'That's enough, guys!' Kunal said loudly over the laughter. He eyed the boy for a brief second before turning away. The bully was a stocky teenager of medium height. Kunal had known him since his senior school days in Lavasa. His name was Nikhil. People called him Nik. Nothing about him was extraordinary except his arrogance.

'Silence, everyone. This is not happening in my class again. If I come to know of any such behaviour, be assured there will be serious consequences,' Professor Rawat tried to restore some order.

*Useless ... all of them ...*

---

After what felt like a long morning, packed with excitement, it was finally time for lunch. Kunal had left with some boys, promising to join Sevita in the canteen later.

'Where is Sama?' Sevita looked around, but she could not find her sister.

'Let her be, Sevita. Maybe she needs some space,' said Astha. Shruti agreed. 'Come and have lunch with us. I am sure she'll join us soon,' she said. Sevita hesitated and looked around a bit more, before joining her friends. Maybe they were right.

---

There was a dense, green patch on a hill, not far from the college building. The more you went up the trail, the colder it felt. Sama walked in the shade of tall, lush trees. She looked around. There was no one on the hill. It was perfect. She sat on a large tree stump, looking at a file of black ants marching around it. They took a detour and went around her feet. She ate her sandwiches, watching them. Once she was done, she stood up and walked back, passing the football court.

'Kunal! Here!'

Sama stopped and turned. Kunal was playing football with some of his friends. She walked towards the court. Sure enough, that was Kunal's backpack lying near a tree. Sama stood and watched him as he played. He was taller than the other boys and the best-looking of them all. His bright brown eyes and chiselled features could draw the world's attention.

Above all, he was kind. He always stood up for her, just as he had done in the class that morning. Over the past two years, she'd watched him closely. There was something about him that made her feel warm inside. A feeling she never got from anything or anyone else.

The match was soon over, and Kunal came running towards his bag. He threw himself on the grass, unscrewed his bottle and gulped some water. Then he poured the rest over his head, shaking the dripping water away from his face.

'It's quite hot for monsoon.'

He turned around, startled.

'Sama! Wow, you scared me.' Kunal wiped the water from his brows. Sama's lips curved into a lopsided smile. She knelt beside him and watched him dry his hair with a small towel.

'You didn't tell the class you like to walk in the woods. Or swim in the river, sometimes,' she said breathlessly. Kunal looked at her in surprise.

'Looks like Sevita talks about me,' he said and looked away, blushing. 'I miss the ocean, so I make do with the river. And I love the hills here.' Sama looked into his childlike eyes. They twinkled with vitality.

'I'm sure you do ... thanks for today.'

'Anytime. You are important to us. We won't let anyone bully you. Just stay away from those jokers. I don't like them,' he said.

'Us?'

'Yes, Sevita and I ... we are family, right?' he said gently, flashing another smile. Sama nodded. Her smile disappeared.

'Anyway, let's go to the canteen. Sevita and the others are waiting.' He grabbed his bag and stood up.

'No, I had my lunch. I don't want to go to the canteen,' Sama said, staring at the grass. There was a file of black ants there too.

'Oh, okay, I'll tell her. See you around!' He waved and walked away.

---

Sama stayed there, watching the ants, her head bent to her right. The angles of the shadows around her changed. Yet Sama didn't move and continued to watch the ants, unaware of the time. In a sudden, impulsive movement, she disrupted the file with her fingers, rubbing aggressively into the mud and grass. The ants went helter-skelter. Their sense of direction was lost.

Evening descended as the first day of college drew to a close. Sama stood up, brushing the mud off her knees and walked towards the parking area. She knew she had missed the lectures after lunch. They must've been boring anyway. Just as Sama reached the parking lot, the final bell rang, and students came rushing out of the college building, chattering and laughing. Sevita and her group of friends came out too. Sama stood silently behind a wall. She would wait for everyone to leave before she walked towards her sister. The group was talking and laughing, making plans to watch a movie. Just then, Kunal joined them. Sama peered from behind the wall to get a better look at him. He looked so fresh and full of life. How wonderful it would be if he talked to her more often. She held on to the edge of the wall tightly, watching them.

'Sevita, umm,' Kunal was saying, rubbing the back of his head and glancing at her sister. 'Can we talk later today?'

Sevita blushed yet again. Shruti looked at the two and made a face. Astha smiled.

'Yeah, why not? Later ...'

Sevita and Kunal communicated through their eyes, a language no one around them could understand. After all, it had been their code for two years now.

Sama stood there, watching. Her nails hurt from gripping the wall too hard. She was perhaps the only other person in the world who knew their code language.

# WRITHING

Sama lay on her bed with her headphones on. She had been in her room since the sisters had returned home from college. She was lost in a memory from ten years ago. It was all so vivid. A little girl, wearing a frilly yellow dress and a matching ribbon in her wind-ruffled ponytail. She was standing in front of their old house in Pune, on a grass patch near the main road. She could still see how the leaves had rustled in the gentle wind as she bent her head sideways and watched. A small puppy, whimpering, dragged a bleeding leg across the road. She watched how the dragging leg left a trail of blood. The puppy was trying to move towards her house. She knew this because it always came inside to play with Sevita. Just then, she heard a shrill scream. Sevita, wearing an identical dress and ribbon, came running across their front garden and knelt near the puppy in the middle of the road.

'Maa! Maa!' she screamed at the top of her lungs. Some neighbours peeked out of their windows. Their mother came rushing out of the house.

'What happened? Oh, oh my God!' she covered her mouth, horrified at the sight of the pup's crushed leg. Sevita was holding it in her arms. Her frock was stained with blood, her eyes red with tears.

'He must've come under a car or something.' Mrs Vyas guided them away from the road and towards the grass patch.

'Take him to a doctor. Please save him!' Sevita cried.

'I'll get the car keys,' their mother said and turned to the house.

'It'll die,' Sama said nonchalantly. 'It's been bleeding for a long time. I don't think there is any blood left inside it at all.'

Sevita cried louder. Mrs Vyas stared at Sama, frightened by her calmness. Ever since that day, their mother had never been the same with her. She had never hugged her or kissed her like she did Sevita.

*She hates you,* a voice hissed in her head.

Sama pulled the headphones off, as if the voice had come from it and stood up. There was a full-length mirror in the corner of her room. She walked up to it and looked at herself. Her face was just the same as Sevita's but without her sister's lively expressions. It was as if the reflection of a hollow ceramic doll was staring back at her. Lifeless and empty.

---

'Maa, I'll be back in a while.'

'Where are you going, Sevita?'

'Just Shruti's place.'

Sama heard Sevita's hurried footsteps. She was wearing heels, probably the pair of red wedge heels she had bought a week ago. She heard the front door shut over the sounds of her dad watching TV in the living room. Sama picked up her black jacket and stepped out of the room quietly.

'I'll be back soon,' she almost whispered to Mr Vyas.

'Hmm ...' He was so immersed in his movie that he did not see Sama take the keys to the scooty when she left.

Sama walked towards where the scooty was parked. A faint light from the street lamps lit the road. She could hear the clacking of her sister's heels at some distance. Suddenly a car's engine came rumbling to life. Then the sound of the heeled footsteps was gone. By the time Sama was on the road, no car was visible, but she knew where to go. It was a path that wound up the hills and into the forest. She didn't wear a helmet as she rode up the hilly road. A cold breeze hit her face as she whizzed past the trees. Slowly the surroundings became darker, the tree growth denser. Sama knew there was a deserted spot close by, near the top of a hill. You had to take a sharp right turn and go off the trail to get there.

A car was parked behind some bushes, just beyond the turn. Sama stopped a good distance before she reached the car and hid the scooter behind a rock. The moonlight was amazingly bright that night. Only the sound of cicadas could be heard. Were they singing or screaming? Sama moved quietly. There were not many sheltered spots there except for a big rock at the very edge of the hill. But she couldn't approach the spot directly without being seen. She took another path towards the same point. It was dangerous, a narrow and muddy trail. After a few minutes, she climbed up behind the big rock at the edge. There was a spot where she could sit down, unseen, and still be within hearing range. She could even watch them from here.

'C'mon, stop it, Kunal!' Sevita was laughing. She was sitting close to him, not far from the edge, looking out over the moonlit landscape. 'Your jokes are not funny anymore.'

'Aren't they? Oh no, seems like you are a college girl now.' He stressed on the word 'college'.

'Yes, that I am. So are you.'

'I'm a college girl?' He joked. Sevita nudged him. Kunal held her arm playfully.

'Let go!' She tried to free her arm but stopped when her eyes met his.

'You said you wanted to wait till we were in college and now we are.' He moved closer to her. 'You know I love you. From the first time I saw you, I have loved you. Will you go out with me? Give me a chance to win you forever?'

With each word she heard, Sama's heart grew colder.

'Yes, I love you too,' Sevita said at last. Kunal let out a small laugh. They inched closer till their lips touched. Sevita trembled as they kissed.

'It's just me,' Kunal whispered, holding her close in a warm embrace. 'Close your eyes ...'

He kissed her again. Sevita put her arms around his neck, caressing his hair and then moving her fingers to his face. They seemed to be swaying together, lost in the moment.

Sama watched them kiss for a long time until both were out of breath. They chuckled together softly. Sevita leaned against Kunal, and he put his arms around her, kissing her on her forehead. It was a night they would never forget.

It was a night Sama could never forget.

---

Sama quietly retraced her way to the scooty and rode home. She went into her room without eating her dinner and lay on her bed, staring at the ceiling. Something was wrong. It was a silent night, and yet her ears rang with weird vibrations. She felt distinctly queasy. She could feel acid pump out of her heart instead of blood. Every inch of her body started to burn.

'No ... no ... Go away!' She rubbed her arms, her chest, her stomach and her head. Finally she stood up, almost tearing her T-shirt off. Then she walked to the mirror and looked at her sorry self. Her hair was messed up, so she combed it down, just like Sevita did every day. Then she cleaned the kajal smeared by her tears. Taking a deep breath, she smiled. But her smile was lopsided. The fact stung her, so she took another deep breath and lifted the other side of her lips deliberately.

'Ha! I look just like her,' she said to her reflection. She tried to mimic her sister's laugh. Her own laugh had a dull, nasal sound, so she cleared her nose and throat and tried again. She practised Sevita's laughter, the way she raised her eyebrows, the way she glanced at Kunal shyly every time she saw him, the way she stood upright with her chin slightly down. She stopped abruptly.

*You can never be her ... try all you want ... this is just you mimicking her.*

She stared into the mirror, her expression back to lifeless.

---

The next morning, Sama announced that she would be taking the bus to college. Sevita and Mr Vyas tried to dissuade her.

'I don't like to ride on a two-wheeler. Besides, I can't wait for your friends to leave every day.'

'You could talk to them, Sama ...'

'I don't like them. I will only speak with Kunal,' Sama said coldly. Then she left for the bus stop, leaving her father and sister dumbstruck. 'I don't know why you bother,' Mrs Vyas said to no one in particular.

Over the week it became clear that this was Sama's new routine. Sevita tried to talk to her, but Sama shut her out, both in college and at home. It seemed as if she did not want to talk to her sister at all. Even Shruti and Astha were concerned, but no one knew how to deal with Sama. Not even her father.

Kunal couldn't bear to see Sevita worrying about Sama every day. 'Let's see, we can take her with us to the movie. What say?' he said to Sevita. 'It's a special screening organized by a friend. I can arrange an extra ticket.'

'That should be good.' Sevita smiled at his suggestion as they sat together in a café.

The word about Sevita and Kunal seeing each other had spread like wildfire. Everyone in college was talking about it. No one cared about the moody twin who disappeared at lunchtime into the forest.

Sama hadn't found an opportunity to follow her sister since that night on the hill. Sevita went out with Kunal every day, often right after classes, so she couldn't follow them. Instead, she took to walking in the forest. She would take a jar with her. The woods presented her with a wide variety of insects. Moths, butterflies, dragonflies, centipedes, cicadas ... every kind of insect people wouldn't want in their homes. She used a small net to catch them and stored them in separate jars. Moths were her favourites. The bigger the better. Insects were so much easier to handle than humans.

---

Saturday arrived, bringing in thunder and rain. Sevita saw the sky turn grey from her window and felt her spirits sink. She wanted to be with Kunal, but the rains made it impossible. She sipped her hot chocolate and sighed, wondering how she would spend the weekend without seeing him. She hoped Monday would bring a clearer sky. As she daydreamed, her phone rang.

'What are you doing?' It was Kunal. He sounded as if he was out in the rain.

'I'm at home watching the downpour and ruing the fact that we will not be able to see each other today.'

'Says who? Open your window.'

'What?' She blinked.

'Open it. Wait, lock your door first.'

'It's locked!' Sevita rushed to open the window. Kunal was standing right outside it beside the hedge.

'Kunal! What are you … Goodness! Come in, quick.' She helped him climb up and jump inside. He had an excited grin on his face as if he'd crossed the Atlantic and reached the shore.

'Pure luck that your room is on the ground floor. Or I would've had to climb a wall,' he said, ruffling his dripping hair.

'You are soaked,' Sevita said, handing him a towel. 'This is such a bad idea. You will catch a cold.'

'Yeah, I should take my shirt off,' he joked. Sevita threw a cushion at him.

'You are really lucky. Dad is out at work, and Mom is busy with her fruit art. Sama is lost as usual in her own world somewhere in her room and—'

Kunal pulled her close and kissed her, taking her by surprise. She closed her eyes as her legs turned to jelly. When he pulled away, she felt her lungs had forgotten to breathe.

'I can't live a day without seeing you,' he looked into her eyes and said. His body was warm against her, even with a barrier of a soaking wet shirt.

Sevita smiled and looked away. Water dripped from his hair onto her face.

'Kunal, you are soaking wet. I guess you should take your shirt off and let it dry. But behave yourself, okay? We will only talk.' She looked at him and pressed a finger against his lips.

'Yes, ma'am!' He smiled and unbuttoned his shirt, revealing a muscular torso. Sevita looked away, turning bright red, and found a hairdryer to dry his shirt. Kunal watched her work diligently. Even while drying a wet shirt she looked gorgeous. To him, she was the most beautiful girl in the world.

Sevita felt Kunal's eyes on her and glanced at him. He was radiating a kind of vigour that made her feel lightheaded. She needed to focus on drying the shirt if she wanted to stay sane.

'This should do for now.' Sevita kept the dryer aside after some time. 'It will dry soon, I guess.' She stepped closer to him, trying not to look into his eyes.

'Don't worry about it,' he said as their fingers intertwined.

'Kunal, we are going too far, too fast. Let's draw a line here,' Sevita said, hesitating, and looked up. Kunal was smiling back at her.

'Yes, we should. We can go as slow as you want. But can I sit inside your blanket for a while? It's cold!' Kunal said.

'Yes, you can,' Sevita laughed. They sat together on a couch beside her bed with a blanket over them, arm in arm, talking about every random topic they could think of. Sevita even sneaked in extra hot chocolate for him.

In the far end of the room across the corridor, darkened by the clouds outside and heavy curtains inside, Sama was sitting on the floor in a corner with her tablet. She peered into the screen and watched Sevita and Kunal as they played thumb wars. She listened as they discussed their date plans. She had a clear view of Sevita's room.

'If the weather clears tomorrow, I will take you to this new café near the water sports club. Nik and his bully gang posted a picture of it. Looks good,' Kunal was saying.

'The one with Italian food? Let's do it,' Sevita replied.

'Delisiozo, yeah. We can also take a speedboat ride.'

'Hmm ... Only if you promise to hold me, or I will fall.'

'I promise. We will go after the movie,' Kunal said, as she leaned over to kiss him.

Alone in her room, Sama watched them kissing and stroking each other. She watched how Kunal's hands glided over Sevita's face, neck and back. She watched as they looked into each other's eyes in peaceful silence. Once again, Sama felt her heart pumping acid. She was unable to breathe properly. If only she could look into his eyes like Sevita did.

# OBSESSION

It was eleven in the morning. Shruti had a large bucket of butter popcorn in her hands. Just carrying it was a task, but her problem was that she didn't have a third hand to eat the popcorn as she waited for the door to Screen 2 to open. Astha was busy on her phone in a corner, and Kunal and Sevita were in a queue to get nachos. Sama stood some distance apart from Shruti, dressed in a black T-shirt and jeans. Sevita looked gorgeous in her white skirt and pink top. She and Kunal had been gazing into each other's eyes, oblivious to all else.

'I'm not coming with these lovebirds for a movie ever again,' Shruti declared as Sevita and Kunal returned with some nachos and drinks.

'Aww,' Sevita raised a handful of popcorn to her friend's mouth. 'Open your mouth, Shru!'

Shruti pretended to snort in disgust. 'Really?' However, she let Sevita feed her.

'I love you too.' Sevita playfully pinched her cheek.

The door to the hall opened. Finally, they could watch *A Winter's Affair*.

'Maybe we should sit in a different row from these two,' Shruti told Astha as they walked behind them. The girls chose an empty row way behind the couple. Sama followed suit. The movie started, and some people whistled. Soon, everyone seemed engrossed in the story unfolding on the screen.

Sama couldn't care less about the plot or the art direction. She watched Sevita and Kunal from the back row, oblivious to the excitement around her. She watched them hold hands and inch closer to each other. Sama couldn't take her eyes off them. The smile on Sevita's face, every expression, the shy gaze ... Sama noticed it all.

'They sure need a room,' Shruti muttered to Astha as she chewed on a mouthful of popcorn. Astha sighed, tired of Shruti's remarks.

The movie ended, and the five exited the hall. Everyone except Sama was discussing their favourite scenes. Shruti was awed by the actress's beauty and Astha by her costumes.

'My favourite part was the fight scene,' Kunal said.

'Mine was the dance. It was just so cool. What about you?' Sevita turned to Sama.

'When they held hands,' she replied blankly.

'Oh! Such a romantic you are, who would've guessed,' Sevita laughed and poked her.

'Okay gang, I've got to be somewhere. See you tomorrow!' Astha gave Sevita and Shruti a quick hug each and left.

'I'm hungry,' Shruti said.

'We're going to check out a new café today,' Kunal said, taking Sevita's hand. 'You could join us.'

'Umm, no thanks. You two carry on. I will go home,' Shruti said, looking away. 'See you later.'

'So, it's just us,' Sevita said, looking at Sama and Kunal.

'I'm not hungry. I'll accompany you to Delisiozo and then take a bus home.'

Sevita blinked in surprise. 'How did you know we were going there?'

'There is only one new café in the area,' Sama replied, holding onto the straps of her handbag tightly.

'Okay, let's go then,' Sevita said. She thought it weird that her twin had guessed the name of the restaurant accurately. She brushed the thought aside. How did it matter anyway?

---

The three got into Kunal's car and drove off, with the car stereo playing some old-school hip hop. As they approached Delisiozo, Kunal and Sevita asked Sama to join them yet again. When she did not relent, they dropped her off near the bus stop. Sama stood there and watched Kunal's car disappear around a turn. Three buses came and left. Sama didn't board any of them. Abruptly she started walking, not knowing why, away from the bus stop. The road led to a riverside locality full of cafés and restaurants. Delisiozo was somewhere in those buildings, on a top floor overlooking the river.

She turned to the river and stared at the big ripples it made. The water level had risen; she could no longer see the lines left by the river on the boundary walls, which were visible in summer. And the monsoons were just beginning. They would be fierce, this time.

At a distance, Lavasa's water sports club was buzzing with activity. It was a two-storeyed building with glass windows, surrounded by trees. Sama noticed people gathered there, a lot of them from her class. She went closer, walking in the shadows of buildings and quickly crossing the road to avoid being spotted. There was a huge banner announcing the

'Lavasa Water Club Speed Boat Racing Competition'. She spotted Nik among the participants. He was all geared up for the race, wearing a helmet and a yellow life jacket over black trunks. He was flexing his muscles at every opportunity. His gang of toadies was there to cheer him on. She watched him walk around, chest puffed out with confidence, as the time for the race drew near.

'Sevita, hey!' Someone tapped her shoulder. Sama turned back with a jolt. The boy realized his mistake immediately.

'Oh, Sama ... Sorry, I thought you were her ...'

It was the guy from class, who had asked what the name 'Sevita' meant. An awkward silence followed. Sama stared at him, feeling acid ooze out of her heart again.

'Why don't you join us for the—' he stopped in the middle of the sentence. Sama had simply walked away from him.

*Fool,* the voice hissed inside her head. She walked fast through the crowd, not caring who she pushed out of her way. *How disappointed he was when he realized I wasn't Sevita.*

Sama boarded the next bus she could find to her house. She got a window seat and spent the rest of the journey staring out of it. The acid in her chest was making her sweat. Whatever it was deep inside, was trying to burst out and escape.

*I'm going to explode, I will be torn apart.* She clutched at the neck of her T-shirt as the voices started to hiss in her head. The bus stopped across from her house, and she quickly walked inside.

Her mother was busy carving watermelons when she reached home. They did not exchange any greetings. Mr Vyas was at work. Sama rushed into her room and locked the door.

The curtains were drawn back, letting light in. She closed them in a hurry, breathless, and rubbed her arms as if to brush off ants crawling on her.

There was only one thing to do now to release all that pain. Sama knelt on the floor beside her bed and drew out some jars from underneath. Moths of different colours and patterns beat their wings against the glass as if trying to escape their impending doom. Then she took an empty glass jar layered with Plaster of Paris and a bottle of ethyl acetate. Sama poured some of the liquid into the layered jar with a dropper. Then she took out a big moth. It fluttered its wings, shedding its scales between her fingers, but couldn't escape. Its colourful scales broke between her fingers and down it went into the poisoned jar.

Sama closed the lid quickly and leaned closer. The moth thrashed its wings helplessly, breaking them off. Soon it stopped moving, except for a few occasional twitches. She took out another moth and put it in the same jar to watch it die. The moth weakened and slowed down, twitching randomly, exposing its underside before going still. Then she put another moth in, and another, and another ...

The chemical didn't seem to be working now, so she took a thin steel wire from under her mattress and slowly pierced a moth's body. It didn't die at once, so she pierced it a few times. However, that didn't satisfy her, so she put drops of ethyl acetate directly on its body. It gave one last try to flap its wings in an attempt to fly, but the poison killed it. Her eyes were wild as she watched the moths die and go still. After killing a dozen moths this way, her breathing was normal again.

'WHAT IS THAT?'

Sama sat up with a jerk. The jar full of dead moths rolled out of her lap and spilled the tiny bodies. Standing at the door, Mrs Vyas screamed at the top of her lungs, 'Sama, answer me! What is that?'

---

Sama stared calmly at her mother. 'Moths.'

Mrs Vyas was visibly shaken. She saw the bottle of ethyl acetate on the floor, jars full of trapped insects and a carpet strewn with dead moths. She was aghast and broke out in cold sweat. Without a word, she grabbed Sama's arm and almost dragged her out of the room. She locked her in another room and called her husband home at once. When he walked in an hour later, she was on the verge of tears, still trembling.

'This girl is *mad*!' Mrs Vyas cried. She took her husband to their daughter's room and showed him the moths. They searched her room and found hundreds of them—some stored in jars, dead, some alive and some pinned on makeshift display boards. Mr Vyas stared at them.

'Shilpa, it's just a hobby. Like yours is fruit carving and stuff. Insect collection is pretty common,' he said. 'She's making displays—'

'It's not a normal thing to do!' His wife cut in. 'I saw her. I saw her! She was putting drops of that poison—' She pointed at the bottle of ethyl acetate, '—on those moths when they were still alive. She was watching them die!' Mrs Vyas was desperate to make her husband understand. She had seen a look in Sama's eyes that she just couldn't bring herself to articulate. 'It's a good thing I noticed she was acting funnier than usual, so I quietly used a spare key to see what she was doing inside her room.'

Mr Vyas looked at his wife, pained. He was staggered by the level of mistrust his wife had for their daughter.

'You spied on her? You have always been too hard on her, I know that. But spying on the girl and locking her in another room, searching her room as if she's a criminal ...?' He stood up angrily, his voice contemptuous.

'Mohan, please, I know what I saw,' she pleaded. 'The look in her eyes was not normal. You have to believe me.' She held his arm.

'You said the same thing when that puppy incident happened.' He shook his head in disbelief and pulled his arm away.

'That wasn't normal either. A child should be more scared at the sight of blood. She wasn't.'

'She wasn't, because she's different.'

'She's abnormal!'

'Shilpa, you have a misconception that both our girls should be the same.' Mr Vyas was fuming now. 'But here's the news; they are not. Accept it. Sama is different.'

'I am not comparing them. She was like that from the start, I know, but there is some problem here.' Mrs Vyas sighed, covering her face as tears rolled down her cheeks. 'I don't feel good around her. She makes me uneasy. Mohan, as a mother, I shouldn't be feeling that.'

Mr Vyas stood still, speechlessly watching his wife cry.

'Shilpa, I've never felt uncomfortable around her, and I'm her father. You have treated her differently since birth. Is it because she put your life in danger?' he asked sorrowfully. His wife looked up at him. An uncomfortable silence fell between them.

During childbirth, Sevita's delivery was without complications, but Sama's neck was entangled in the placenta. Bringing her into the world had put Mrs Vyas's life at stake.

Maybe he was right. Maybe she had, somewhere in her subconscious mind, hated Sama for putting her life at risk. Her shoulders dropped as she yielded to her husband's logic.

'I just can't put a finger on what is wrong. Maybe it *is* me,' she said, rubbing her eyes. Mr Vyas put his arms around her and comforted her.

'I know she's not the easiest person, but everything will be all right with time. Don't worry. Let's throw all this stuff out, except for the displays she has made. I will get her proper equipment for her hobby so she won't have to use acid on them, okay? It's unsafe for her too.' He smiled at his wife.

---

'Sama, I never knew you had an interest in insect collection. Do you want to study biology?' Mr Vyas asked. Sama was currently enrolled in an engineering course.

'No,' Sama replied without looking at him. Mr Vyas put an arm around her and looked at his wife, willing her to say something.

'Sama, I'm sorry for reacting like I did. It's just that ... killing insects is ... it doesn't feel good to see all that.'

'I see,' Sama replied. 'Do not enter my room again.' She finally raised her eyes to look at her mother. A chill ran down Mrs Vyas's spine.

'I only wanted to make sure you were okay,' she said as calmly as she could.

'No, you did it to spy on me.' A flicker of anger lit her eyes as she stared at her mother.

'Sama, your mom is saying she's sorry. She was worried about you. I think we need to forgive each other.' Mr Vyas raised his brows to stress his point. Sama looked at her father, her eyes expressionless again. Mrs Vyas was taken aback by the sudden change in her expression. Had she imagined it?

'If you say so ...'

'Great! I will get you the right equipment for your hobby. Let's go together to the dam one of these days. There are many water insects there that you can sweep up with a net.' He smiled at her.

'Okay ...,' Sama said, a small lopsided smile at the corner of her lips.

Mrs Vyas stood silently against a wall.

---

'Oh!' Sevita said when her father told her what had happened. 'No wonder she ventures out into the forest on her own. She goes to collect moths. Phew! At least she has a hobby. And now I see why she didn't talk about it in class. People would just make more fun of her.'

'More?' Mr Vyas frowned.

'Well, Nik and some of his cronies made it to our college, same class.' Sevita pouted. 'He's added more apes to his group to make things worse.'

'Those bastards,' Mr Vyas cursed under his breath. 'Talk to the authorities if they harass her again. And call me immediately. Those clowns put her through enough grief in high school.'

'Yes, don't worry.' Sevita patted his arm.

'What's brewing?' Mrs Vyas walked into the hall, carrying a huge plate of fruit salad. It was a beautifully designed platter with all kinds of carved fruits and a whipped cream topping. She had arranged them in a clever 3-D geometric design. Father and daughter sprang up to grab some.

'No!' She slapped their hands away. 'First, I will post a picture on my Instagram. I need to get more orders!'

Sevita and her dad cribbed while Mrs Vyas posted the picture. As soon as she was done, they attacked the salad, relishing the whipped cream on top and the custard inside. It tasted like heaven.

'I'll go give some to Sama,' Sevita said. She took a serving to her sister's room and knocked. The door opened slightly.

'What?' There was a tinge of anger in Sama's voice.

'Fruit salad from Mom! It's a gesture of peace.' Sevita grinned. Sama stared at the plate, took it without a word and shut the door. Sevita was used to her sister's moods, and so she turned to leave.

'Sevita ...?' The door opened again slightly. Sevita turned in disbelief. This was something unique, her twin calling her by her name!

'Yeah?'

'Any plans for the night?'

'Oh, nothing's certain,' she said, looking away.

*Liar ...*

'I see,' Sama said before closing the door again, leaving Sevita baffled.

---

It was eleven. Sevita was sitting beside her window, her cheek pressed to the glass. A single bedside lamp lit her room.

She felt bad for having lied to Sama, but this was a secret she couldn't tell her. Soon enough, there was a knock on the glass. Kunal had come! A broad smile lit up her face as she opened the window and let him in. He had become so adept at climbing in over the past few nights that he could do it without much help now. Sevita put her arms around him.

'What were you getting for me?' she asked him, quickly closing the window. 'You said you have a gift for me?'

'This.' Kunal held out a small gift. Sevita bit her lip and took it. She scanned the prettily wrapped box with a ribbon at the top, turning it around in her hands, and opened it carefully. A beautiful heart-shaped locket sat on a little red cushion inside.

'Go on, open it,' Kunal whispered, bending close to her ear and causing her skin to tingle. Sevita opened the locket. There was a picture of them on one side.

'Why is the other side blank?' she asked, smiling as if she knew the answer.

'There'll be a picture of us there after you marry me,' he declared. 'After college, of course. Once I propose to you properly.'

She smiled brightly, thinking back to an afternoon when they had talked about how their lives would be once they were together forever. Then she looked away, blushing.

'I still have our picture from when we first met, when I wrote my phone number on your hand, and you wrote yours on the back of that picture. That was the day when you first called me. We talked for hours,' she said.

He stepped closer as they stood beside the window. It had started to rain. A storm threatened to smash the window panes.

'Yeah, I wrote my number on the picture so that you couldn't say you didn't recognize the caller. Can I see it?' He asked as his lips brushed against hers, and then over her neck.

'It's always with me, like a lucky charm ...' She closed her eyes and surrendered to the sensation of his lips on her skin, moving down from her neck towards her chest. He gently pushed her towards the bed, and she lay there as his hands caressed her waist, slipping further down. She could feel his body press against hers. All the boundaries seemed to fade. Just then, Kunal moved his hands away from her and dug his head into the pillow beside her.

'I keep losing control with you. I'm sorry,' he whispered, breathing heavily.

'So do I.' She brushed his hair with her fingers. 'It's just that it's better to have some boundaries for now. You understand, right?'

'Yeah, I do.' He pecked her cheek with a small kiss and lay beside her, gazing into her eyes.

'You are so beautiful.'

Sevita chuckled.

They talked for hours, lying side by side, playing with each other's fingers. Sama saw it all, right from the moment he had started to kiss Sevita. She had a little eye in the corner of the ceiling. There was also a microphone on the side of Sevita's bed, but they were speaking too softly for her to hear. It was only when Kunal finally left that she switched her tab off. She reached under her bed and grabbed a glass jar. She took a live moth out and pinned it alive on a display board, piercing its thorax. Then, she took out another and pinned its wings, waiting and watching till it stopped moving and died.

---

From the next day, classes picked up speed as Prof. Rawat, or Mr Oogway as the students called him, started computer programming. Sevita would rigorously take notes in his classes and sit with Kunal during lunch break to try and understand programming. It was one subject that stressed her out, but Kunal seemed to have got the hang of it.

Sama would sit alone in the classroom as always and disappear at lunchtime. The classes were too slow-paced for her. She had mastered many programming languages on her own a long time ago. No subject was difficult for her, and she could learn anything without guidance. It was with this self-acquired expertize in computers that she was able to set up her web of little cameras and microphones anywhere she wanted without being noticed.

After one such boring lecture, Sama slipped out, as silent as still air. The patch of woods behind the college building had become her preferred retreat. The rotting stump belonged to her. Ants would still make a file and march around her, even though she scratched their path out every day. *What a pity! They never learn,* she thought and quietly ate her sandwiches, watching them run helter-skelter.

'So that is where you run off to.' Sama heard a brash voice behind her. She turned and saw Nik strut uphill towards her. Three of his gang members followed him with cocky grins.

'Do you know what happens to weird girls like you who go off into the woods alone?' He stretched the word 'alone', smirking. He advanced slowly towards her, as his cronies snickered in the background.

Sama stood still. She didn't know what he was planning to do, but it certainly wasn't good. She moved closer to the stump, feeling her heartbeat become louder. Nik's cronies cackled, making fun of how she stood stiff with terror. Sama's eyes were fixed on him as he approached, flexing his shoulders and popping his knuckles.

*One quick move is all it would take. How much would it hurt?*

# DESIRE

Nik's eyes glazed over as he moved closer to Sama. She stared back at him, her feet planted on the ground.

'Such dead eyes you have, Sama. Let me light them up for you.'

He was only a few steps away, the curl of his lips turned nastier.

One movement was all it would take. She could see the silver gleam of the butter knife inside her lunchbox, open on the stump.

*How much would a man suffer if a butter knife went through his throat?*

Her hands twitched and tingled. A sudden flicker in her eyes made Nik freeze. Did he imagine it or was there a mean glint in Sama's eyes? Whatever it was made him stop in fear.

'Nik!' A loud, angry roar echoed through the woods. Nik and his gang looked around in shock and confusion to see Kunal, striding up the hill, fuming in rage.

'Go back to your girlfriend,' Nik snarled. 'It's none of your business—'

Before Nik could even complete his sentence, everything went black. He hit the ground within seconds, unable to breathe through all the blood spurting out of his nose. His sidekicks leapt forward and held Kunal back from throwing another knock-out punch, this time at the side of his head. Sama had never seen him so livid. It took all three of Nik's cronies to stop him.

'Kunal, relax! He wasn't going to hurt her. It was just plain scare tactics. Let it go, man!'

Kunal uncurled his fists and freed himself, breathing hard, and staring them down. They stepped back.

'Take this piece of shit away. Never come near her again. I'm warning you.' Kunal's voice dropped menacingly low. They picked up a half-conscious Nik and hauled him away as fast as possible. Kunal grabbed Sama's hand and dragged her along, still fuming.

---

'You are not wandering off alone from now on. Is that understood?' Kunal said without looking at her.

'I won't.' She felt the heat emanate from his palm. His grip was strong. Her gaze was fixed on his face, as he pulled her across the campus ground, back to the college building. His ear was visibly red. She let him drag her all the way till they were inside the classroom.

The other students stared as Kunal marched in with Sama and took his seat. The grave expression on his face kept everyone from even asking what had happened.

Sama sat down and looked at Kunal from her corner. Something other than acid was pumping through her veins, something uncontrollable. She could feel the veins pulsate in her left hand, which had been grasped by Kunal just moments ago.

Sevita felt a jolt when she saw Kunal and her sister, but she realized something serious would have happened; Kunal rarely behaved like that. She knew he wouldn't speak about it while others were around.

It was late at night when Sevita finally asked him about it. They were sitting together on the couch in her room. He told her everything, still appalled by what had happened.

'I don't know what would've happened if I had not reached the spot … if you hadn't asked me to find her—' He turned and looked at her seriously.

'Kunal …' She took his right hand and caressed it. The skin over his knuckles was raw from the impact of the punch. 'Thank you so much for taking care of her.' She kissed the reddish patch and cupped his hand in hers. Kunal let out a deep sigh and hugged her.

The tab slipped from Sama's hands. The tactile memory of Kunal dragging her down the hill was burnt into her wrist. She could still feel his heat. Breathless, she stood up in a daze. There were voices in her head, whispering and hissing, as she stood in front of the full-sized mirror.

*Why not me?*

It was all she could ask the reflection in the mirror. The reflection, a distorted image of her own, looked back at her quietly.

---

The weekend came early to Lavasa as heavy rains rode across the hills on storming winds. Every door in the city was closed on Friday morning.

'Sorry, my darling girl.' Mr Vyas hugged Sama and picked up a heavy raincoat. 'We will go out to the woods once the weather is bearable again. I have to be at the dam for some days. The repairs are not complete and in this rain the situation is vulnerable.' He went to work, leaving Sama alone in the living room. Sevita was sitting gloomily in her room, watching the rain that had made it impossible for Kunal to drive over from the other side of the town. Their mother was engrossed in her fruit art, clueless that Sama, wearing her raincoat and rubber boots, was about to set out in the rain.

Sama went into the woods nearby, clutching her new insect net. Mr Vyas, true to his word, had got her some fancy equipment for her 'hobby'. Kunal was not coming anyway, so there was nothing for her to do in her room. It was raining hard, and her boots were sinking ankle-deep in the mud. The further she walked into the woods, the murkier it got. There was an abandoned house in the distance that she often visited. Moths hid in its dark, humid corners. They were an easy catch. Today, however, it seemed someone had already occupied the place.

Hearing voices, Sama stopped not far from the house and stepped behind a tree. She moved closer, noiselessly, till she was within hearing range. To her surprise, it was Astha, sitting with a guy Sama had never seen before. He was tall and lanky and had curly hair that covered his forehead. He looked old enough to be a senior-year college student. His arms were wrapped around Astha's small body. The only way she could have sneaked out of her house that day, Sama deduced, was by lying that she was going to college.

'I'm scared for us, Andrew, really scared. My family would not agree to us being together. Plus, if they come to know about this ...' Astha sighed.

'Hey, don't you trust me? I am doing all of this for us. There's good money in it. Plus, I will get placed latest by next year, and then I can talk to your family.'

He spoke in a husky voice, sniffing and rubbing his nose. Astha looked at his gaunt face. He hadn't been into these substances when she had fallen in love with him.

'You should have never gotten into this,' she said. Her voice was quivering in agony and anger. 'This is not something you can just get out of ... '

'Astha, hey, come here.' He pulled her close. 'I promise I will stop. I will stop the business too. Just give me till this December.'

'No, no, that's too long.' Astha sat up again and shook her head.

'Okay, okay. I will stop now, promise. It's just that I need more money for us.' He tucked her hair behind her ear, stroking her face.

'There are proper ways to do that, Andrew. Once you are placed, the money will come. Then it won't be so tough to persuade them. Promise me you won't continue this.'

She pleaded with him, holding his long hands that were more bones than flesh.

'I promise. Anything for you.' He kissed her.

Sama crouched behind a shrub and watched. Even for her, it was a shock that Astha was seeing a guy. She belonged to a very powerful and conservative family. How did they ever meet?

*That scum hid her dirt so well ... that's applaudable*, she thought and grimaced.

'Andrew, I just want us to be together, always.'

Sama saw their hands intertwine as they kissed. She turned away, flashes of that afternoon with Kunal causing her head to hurt. Had it lasted for hours or just minutes? She did not know. The rain was getting heavier, growing into a thunderstorm. It was only when she saw Andrew leading Astha out of the cottage, under the cover of his raincoat, that she came back to her senses. Once they had left, she quietly emerged from her hiding place and walked away.

---

Back in her room, Sama stood in front of her mirror. Water dripped from her clothes and hair. She was trembling with cold, but that did not stop the hissing voices inside her head or the acid burning her ribcage from within. It was suffocating. There were no moths left in her jars.

'Oh no, why did you come today?' A familiar voice sounded from the tab which lay on the floor. She knelt beside it, watching Sevita as she frantically dried Kunal with a towel. He was dripping wet.

'Because I'm not in town this weekend. If I hadn't come, I wouldn't get to see you till Monday.'

'Kunal, this is dangerous! Did you see the trees that have fallen in the storm? The rain is just too heavy to drive. What if something happened to you? What if there was a landslide and you got stuck? What if someone came from the wrong side and—'

'Hush,' Kunal said, as he placed a finger on her lips. 'I'm here, and I'm fine. I can't leave without seeing you. Don't worry about me so much.' He leaned close to kiss her.

'I can't not worry about you,' Sevita said before putting her arms around him and closing her eyes. She wanted to savour every sensation that came from being close to him.

Sama pushed the tab away. A wildfire spread inside her body. Her head hurt. The hissing voices came back, making no sense at all. Her breathing became erratic.

*Cursed ... you are cursed ... you are not enough ... never be happy ... lifeless ... just a copy ...*

'Stop! Stop!' She clutched at her hair.

It was torture. The splitting pain in her head made it worse. Nothing made sense anymore. Sama slapped her hands over her ears, pressing them hard against the sides of her head, and curled up on the floor in a corner of her room.

For the next two days, she wouldn't go out to eat or drink, and she wouldn't open the door of her room. Her mirror stood like a haunted object. Her room was dark, as dark as her heart. Sama stayed in the corner with her hands over her ears, but the voices would not stop.

Her mother did not dare to check on her. She simply stayed away. Sevita tried to talk to her sister, but that was the last thing Sama wanted—to look at the face that was just like hers, but with life. It was only at night when everyone was asleep that Sama would come out. There would always be some dinner kept aside for her every night, but that only made Sama angrier. She threw away the food and ate anything else that she could find.

The voices were getting louder by the hour. They seemed to follow her everywhere. Sometimes they seemed to be coming from the walls of the house, so clear and real did they sound.

Sama sat for hours on the couch at night with her arms wrapped around her knees, watching the wall clock tick and the moonlight shift the shadows of the drawing room. The rains never stopped. The voices didn't either. Even the roaring thunder couldn't muffle them. Now they were taking shape on the walls of the house. Wherever she looked, she saw swirling shadows and distorted faces. She saw eyes and mouths appear on the walls.

At dawn on Monday, the rain stopped. The clouds were still heavy but white. There was mist over the river, which was splashing against its banks. Sama hadn't slept the night before. She quietly went to her room early in the morning and dressed for college. Before locking her room, she looked around at it. The heavy curtains were drawn. No clothes lay outside, and no pictures hung on the wall. Her laptop was placed neatly on her study table. There was nothing that hinted at the mess in her mind.

The most beautiful thing in there was her mirror. The full-length, oak-framed mirror stood against a wall, its clear surface gleaming. Her reflection looked back with an empty expression.

At a quarter to seven, she was sitting on the couch in the living room where she had spent the previous two nights when Sevita came out of her room. She was wearing a white top, denim shorts and sneakers.

'Sama ...,' She stopped when she saw her sister in the drawing room. Apprehension was writ large on her face; she wanted to ask her sister what was wrong but didn't know how she would react. Why couldn't she ever figure out Sama's thoughts?

'Good morning,' Sama said.

Sevita bit her lip and looked out of the window, feeling her heart twist. Sama got up to leave. The college bus was going to arrive any moment now.

'Wait, Sama,' Sevita said. 'Let's go together today, please? I want to talk to you. Sister to sister.'

Sama watched the expressions on Sevita's face. How easily her brows came together in worry, how softly her eyes looked into her own, how her lips quivered ever so slightly as she sighed and bit her lip, how her fingers gripped a chair in nervous agitation ...

'Why?'

'Just because.' Sevita came closer and took Sama's bag. Then she held her twin's hand. Her grip was soft and gentle, warm against Sama's cold hands. 'See you after college, Mom! We're leaving.'

'Oh, you're going together?' Mrs Vyas asked from inside her room.

'Yeah, bye!' Sevita waved and walked out of the house with Sama. They were on the road in five minutes.

# TRIGGER

The air was damp and cold as they rode down the coiling road. The wind blew hard, making the clouds look like white ghost ships. The hills were a lush, cool shade of dark green. The landscape was hauntingly beautiful.

They were now crossing the bridge over the rioting river. Sama watched the strong waves as they beat against the iron pillars, layer upon layer. The storm was just taking a break.

Midway on the bridge, Sevita slowed down and stopped the scooter. She parked on the side and got off. Sama followed suit, reluctant at first. Sevita took her helmet off and drew a long, deep breath. She stretched her arms and looked up at the shifting clouds.

'Such beautiful weather today, don't you agree?' She turned to Sama who simply stared at her. 'Look at the golden light rising up slowly behind the clouds ... We should come here and observe nature together more often—'

'What is this about?' Sama asked, her tone brittle. Sevita bit her lip hesitantly as she leaned against the railing of the bridge.

'Sama, we don't talk much. But we're sisters, twins at that. We may have been born to lead different lives, but you and I started life together. I think we should understand each other the best, but you never tell me what's on your mind. You never talk about anything.' She gazed into Sama's eyes, careful not to probe too deep. 'Not about that day with Mom, or about what happened last week ... *anything*.'

'There is nothing to tell,' Sama said curtly.

'There's a lot to tell.' Sevita dropped her voice, 'These past two days, you shut yourself in. I know you have been throwing away the food I kept for you. Talk to me about it. What's on your mind, Sama?'

A sharp intake of breath, and the wildfire inside Sama erupted in her eyes.

'It's always you ... everywhere,' Sama snapped.

Sevita felt as if she had been struck by lightning. Yes, it was always her, from their earliest childhood, for as long as she could remember. Sama had been pushed aside by their mother and by other people.

'I am nowhere,' Sama continued.

Silence followed, broken only by the howling wind.

'That's not true,' Sevita said, shaking her head. 'You are here. You are a part of me, and I am a part of you. We were together before we were even born, and we are together now. It's people who differentiate between us. But we know better. It doesn't matter what they—'

'It matters a lot to me.' The pool of acid inside Sama started to surge again. The cool atmosphere around her was no comfort.

'I understand that it's difficult. You have always faced adversities,' Sevita cried as she stepped closer and took her sister's hands.

'Someone like you cannot understand me.' Sama pulled her hands away, frowning.

'Try me. Tell me anything and everything. Hell, you can ask me for whatever you want,' Sevita said with a smile.

They stood close together, facing each other. It was as if they were staring at their own reflections.

'Whatever I want?'

'Yes, anything. I know people compare us. And yes, we are different. But on the inside, we are one, you and I. Just look into the mirror, and you will see me.'

'Same in the mirror ...'

'We are, aren't we?'

Sama's frown melted away. She looked intently at her twin. Sevita felt they were finally coming to an understanding; the terseness in Sama's voice was vanishing.

'We should have been one. I wish I could be like you.' Sama's voice was soft, vulnerable. Sevita could see Sama open up for the first time in seventeen years.

'You don't have to be like me. Just be as different as you are and as special.'

Finally, Sevita felt she was getting through to Sama. Her sister wanted to make friends too, but it was hard for her because of her introverted nature.

'Yeah ... maybe I don't have to be like you because we are one already.'

Sama's lips curved into a lopsided smile. Sevita smiled back. It was the start of a good dialogue.

'This is just the beginning, Sama.' Sevita took another deep breath, turning and looking up at the morning clouds. She held the railing of the bridge. The wind was swift, sweeping the dark clouds across the sky.

'But then, if we are one, there should be just one of us.'

Sevita blinked, a frown appearing on her forehead. Did she hear Sama right? She sounded weird, almost as if she were a different person. Sevita turned around.

'What do you—'

Sevita stopped. The look in Sama's eyes wasn't normal. Her heart pounded in warning, but her body froze in fear.

The next second, all she could see were the dark, rumbling clouds. Her feet were no longer on the ground. Her chest hurt and her head hit something. Everything went black. She didn't feel the icy waves forcing her body along the current, away from the bridge and the town.

---

The wind was picking up speed.

Sama flexed her fingers. They were warm from pushing Sevita off the bridge in a brutal thrust. It was impulsive. The exertion had made her blood flow with renewed vigour. She watched her twin bob up and down with the waves. Sometimes her white top was visible before it was covered in steel-grey water again. She seemed to be drowning fast, her body limp and powerless. Sama blinked.

'What did you do, Sama ...'

Her brows came together in worry. She bit her lips as they quivered ever so slightly. Her eyes widened in sorrow and filled with tears.

'Why did you do this, Sama? You jumped!' Tears rolled down her cheeks. 'Right in front of my eyes, and I couldn't stop you! God ... what do I do?'

She rushed to the scooter and took Sevita's bag out of the back box. Finding her phone, she hurriedly tapped a number.

'Kunal?' she sobbed into the phone, her voice shrill and breathless.

'Sevita? Hey, what's wrong?' he asked.

'I stopped on the bridge for a while with Sama ... we were just talking, I ... I didn't know ...'

'What didn't you know? What happened?'

'She … Sama … she jumped off the bridge!'

'WHAT?'

'Kunal … she's gone!'

There was a shocked silence.

'Stay there. I am coming. Please just stay there.' Kunal's voice was shaking. 'Don't do anything. Just stay on the bridge. Sit down and wait for me. I'm coming.'

Sama did what he asked. She sat on the scooty that Sevita had parked next to the railing. Then a thought came to her mind. If Kunal were to see her in these clothes, a loose black top over skinny jeans, he would have his doubts. Sevita never dressed like this. She stood up instantly, kick-started the scooty and rode back home as fast as she could.

Sama always kept the windows of her room unlocked behind the heavy curtains to have a secret route in and out of the house. She entered quietly and made her way to Sevita's room—a room full of colours and life. The walls were covered with posters of her favourite bands and celebrities, quotes, pictures and collages. Her table was strewn with travel magazines, novels, make-up and gadgets. Sama quickly opened her sister's cupboard and pulled out a pair of shorts and a white top. She changed into them.

'Hello, I need to order some fruits. Are you delivering today?' Mrs Vyas was busy on her phone in the hall. Sama noiselessly crossed the corridor and went into her room. She dumped the clothes she had been wearing that morning in a corner of her cupboard and made a silent exit the way she had come in.

She realized that Kunal must have reached the spot by now. That would require a change in her plans. There was only one way.

'Maa …' Her expressions changed again. Tears rolled out and her face contorted in anguish. By the time she went around to the front door, it was drizzling. She ran towards the door of the house and banged it, shouting.

'Maa! Maa! Open the door! Maaaa!'

'What happened?' Mrs Vyas came rushing out, still in her nightdress. 'Goodness gracious, my baby!' she exclaimed as her daughter hugged her tight and sobbed. Sama's knees gave way, and her body trembled. Mrs Vyas had to lean against the doorway to hold her. She rubbed her daughter's back, asking what happened.

'Maa … Sama … I couldn't save her … She jumped off the bridge!'

'What are you saying?' Mrs Vyas shrieked. Her blood ran cold.

At that moment, Kunal arrived. He jumped out of his car, leaving the door open, and ran towards her.

'Kunal!' Sama saw him run towards her with a face she would never forget. He looked worried and scared but thankful at the same time, to see her unharmed.

'Sevita, please tell me you are okay?' Kunal said.

Sama shook and sobbed harder, holding Mrs Vyas tightly.

Kunal sighed, rubbing his forehead as if it would alleviate the sharp pain there. Tears welled up in his eyes. He pulled his phone out, trying to breathe normally, and called the police.

'I need to report an incident …'

---

Fifteen minutes later, red beacons flashed, and sirens echoed through the hills as police vans and jeeps raced to the bridge. Sama, who had comfortably slipped into Sevita's skin, was sitting beside Kunal in his car, wrapped up in his jacket.

Tears were still rolling down her face. Her mother was in the back seat, her arms limp, trying to make sense of what had happened. Mr Vyas was on his way back from the dam.

The police vehicles braked to a stop, some distance away from Kunal's car. Two policemen set about sealing the area with yellow tape. Their plastic head covers fluttered ferociously in the wind. A tall, thin man with broad shoulders stepped out of a car. Some men saluted him. He looked around as if to survey the scene. In weather like that, it would be next to impossible to collect any evidence, let alone search for a body.

'Let's talk to the witness first,' he commanded, loud and clear, over the accelerating wind. One of his subordinates stepped forward and led him to Kunal's car. Kunal rolled the window down. The police officer was imposingly tall. His black raincoat made him all the more intimidating.

'Inspector Suresh Mohite,' he said, leaning close to the window and showing his ID card. 'I need to ask her a few questions. Your cooperation at this time is crucial.' Kunal nodded and turned to look at the woman he thought was his girlfriend. He had never seen her so sad. Her hands had never felt so cold to his touch. She wasn't speaking anymore, or even looking at anyone.

'Sevita ...' He slipped his palm under her icy hands. She looked at him. 'Please tell us everything. What happened?'

She nodded, wiping her tears on the sleeve of his jacket and sniffing. 'We were standing here in the middle of the bridge ... I had stopped there ... just to talk to her ... about all that was going on. I had no clue what she was going to do.'

'What was going on?' the inspector asked, piercing her with his sharp eyes.

---

'She was bullied recently ... and wasn't talking to anyone after that incident.'

'Who bullied her?'

'A college mate. Nik. Kunal stopped him before he could do any harm, but she was affected. Scared.'

'How do you know she was scared?'

'She had shut herself inside her room for two days and refused to talk.'

'For two days a member of your family was inside a locked room, and you did not attempt to break in?'

'She hated when we opened the door with the spare key.' Her eyes flickered, for a split second, in anger. 'It would have upset her even more. She was my sister. I knew her better than anyone else.'

'Okay, so what happened this morning?' The inspector's baritone deepened. He leaned closer to the window.

'I stopped the scooter on the bridge to talk to her about the incident at college. I wanted her to relax while we enjoyed the view. I told her that she could depend on me.' Her voice changed, striking a more vulnerable note. Her gaze fell softly on the inspector's face. 'Then, just when I thought she was cheering up, I turned to look at the clouds ... and suddenly I heard a splash. She had jumped—' She broke down, sobbing uncontrollably. 'I couldn't save her!'

Kunal put his arms around her and drew her to him. 'I think that should do for now, sir,' he said. The inspector nodded.

'I will need to question you all again. Please keep my card.' He handed a black and white visiting card to Kunal. His name, designation and number were on it.

The inspector straightened his raincoat and covered the distance to the bridge in swift, long strides.

Kunal patted Sama's head, whispering, 'Everything will be okay. I'm with you.'

She clutched his shirt, pressing her face against his chest. 'You are here, and that's all I need.' A lopsided smile spread on her face through the tears, hidden from Kunal's view.

---

Word spread fast. Everyone in college came to know of the suicide. They whispered about it in the classroom, discussed it during the break. Social media went into a frenzy over the incident. Astha and Shruti were shocked.

'I could never have imagined she would do this. I always thought she was weird, but I had no idea she was struggling,' Shruti said. She felt bad for not having made more of an effort to get to know Sama.

'It was as if … she never existed. I wonder what went through her mind,' Astha said, shaking her head sadly.

'We need to be with Sevita. It must be hard for her,' Shruti mumbled, sipping her coffee. 'She's lucky to have Kunal support her through this time, but as her friends, we should also console her.'

They went to Sevita's house after lunch, skipping their afternoon classes. Silence had fallen over the Vyas residence. Mr Vyas was sitting outside in a corner of his garden, all alone. He had cried himself to exhaustion; his eyes were swollen and red. There were some policemen standing near the gate beside their vehicles.

Astha nudged Shruti and pointed towards a group of people buzzing with cameras and mikes. They stood at a distance, blocked by the policemen on guard. The girls were allowed inside after showing their college IDs. Kunal's car was parked inside the garage, where Mr Vyas's driver was walking to and fro, disturbed by the events of the day.

Who wouldn't be?

The two girls found their legs weakening as they approached the house. How would they face Sevita? What would they say to her? They walked up the cobblestone path across the lawn and reached the front door. It was open.

Sevita was sitting on the bed, with her arms around her knees, her hair strewn around her shoulders, a blank stare on her face. Kunal was with her. Mrs Vyas was sitting on the bedside couch, looking outside.

'You came,' Sama said, her voice barely a whisper.

Shruti stood still, at a loss for words. Astha sighed and sat on the bed beside her. She put her arms around Sama.

'I am sorry,' Astha felt her heart getting heavy with grief as she spoke the words. Shruti also sat next to Sama and took her hand. It was so cold that it startled her, so she tried to rub some warmth into it.

'Sevita, please take care of yourself. I know it's hard, but there is nothing you could've done,' Shruti said softly.

Kunal got some water for the girls and Mrs Vyas. He then went to check on Sevita's father. Sama watched him through the window as he quietly sat with her dad.

Shruti and Astha were consoling her, rubbing her hands and pleading with her to drink some water. It felt good. All these people who didn't care before were concerned about her now. She stayed silent, looking grief-stricken, and let them fuss over her. The clock ticked steadily and soon night fell. Finally, Astha and Shruti left after getting Sama to agree to eat something. Mrs Vyas was leading her cold and weary husband to their room. He hadn't moved from the garden all day.

'I am leaving now but will see you very soon,' Kunal said and bent to kiss her forehead. A wild pulse ran through her.

'Don't leave me alone,' Sama said. She tugged on his sleeve.

'No, I won't.' Then Kunal spoke through his eyes the way he always did with Sevita. Sama understood what he meant. After saying good night to Mrs Vyas, Kunal left by the front door only to return to her through her window.

Sama was waiting beside Sevita's window, her cheek pressed to the glass and eyes searching the darkness outside. A single bedside lamp glowed, casting a dim yellow light. That was just how she used to do it. In ten minutes, Kunal's figure appeared at the window. Sama opened it, and he jumped inside. With a heavy sigh, he took her in his arms.

'I wanted to do this the moment I saw you. Sorry, I couldn't,' he told her.

Sama could feel the warmth not just of his arms around her, but of his whole body. She could feel his breath on her neck. Her pulse quickened. She put her arms around him and pressed her face against his chest.

'Come, you must be exhausted.' He took her gently to her bed and made her lie down, tucking her blanket around her. 'I knew something was not right,' he said, sitting beside her on the bed.

'What do you mean?'

'When I left on Friday, I knew something was going to go wrong. I wish I had stayed with you.' He looked at her with a soft gaze. Sama couldn't control her heartbeat. Those eyes were only hers to look at from that day onwards. Those beautiful, twinkling brown eyes full of warmth and life.

'Nothing would have changed. Don't be hard on yourself,' she said and held his warm hand.

'I don't know ...'

'I know. She had been a recluse for such a long time. No one could have helped her.' She looked at him wistfully. A slight crease appeared between her eyebrows.

Kunal took some time to react. Sevita was hopeful and optimistic, usually. He would have expected her to say the opposite. Then he sighed. How could she be optimistic any longer when the person she wanted to save was gone?

'You tried, Sevita. I saw you agonize over her problems every day,' he said as he caressed her face and stroked her hair.

'Just stay close to me.' She put her hands on his chest. She could feel his heartbeat. It made her feel short of breath. Being close to him was exhilarating.

He stayed by her side all night. Only when Mrs Vyas knocked on the door at 7 a.m. and pleaded with her to join them for tea, did he kiss her hand and leave, promising to see her soon.

---

The college had declared a holiday in Sama's memory, after holding a prayer meeting for her. Everyone, be it the teachers or students, was shocked. They had sensed that she wasn't normal, but how could they have known she would take such an extreme step? The local police station was, meanwhile, abuzz with activity.

'I need surveillance reports, on the double!' Inspector Mohite shouted the command as he entered the Lavasa police station, handing his dripping umbrella and raincoat to a peon. A glance from his razor-sharp eyes was enough to put his subordinates to work in an instant. They were galvanized into action the moment he entered the workspace.

'Sir!' The station's sub-inspector, Vijay Gadre, saluted him. 'The report will be here in some time. But I have another report for you.'

'What other report?'

'It is based on my observation; I was the first to reach the scene.'

'Take me through the events from the top,' Mohite said. He beckoned a new recruit, Vikrant Singh, to join them. They entered his cabin.

Inspector Mohite sat down at his desk, opened a sleek laptop placed beside a neat pile of files and pushed the start button.

'So,' he said, pointing towards the chairs facing his desk. The two men sat down, their backs straight.

'We got a call at exactly 8.16 a.m., sir. It was from a boy named Kunal Mehta. He informed us that a girl named Sama Vyas had jumped off the Lavasa bridge roughly thirty minutes before he made the call. He also told us that the twins Sevita and Sama were on their way to college and had stopped en route on Lavasa bridge when the incident occurred. We arrived at the scene at about 8.45 a.m. The boy wasn't there, so we called him. He had gone to find Sama's sister at her residence. He then brought the sister, Sevita, and her mother to the scene. The girl was in no condition to talk to us. You arrived at the scene not long after, at around 9.15 a.m.'

'Why were you not able to question her?'

'The girl wouldn't leave Kunal. She held onto him. I think she was in shock.'

'You think, or you know?'

'Sorry, sir?'

'Explain how you concluded that she was in shock.'

'Er...,' Gadre adjusted himself on his chair to sit a little straighter. 'I showed them my ID and said I needed to question them. Record statements. But she wouldn't speak at all, or even react when I addressed her by name. She hid her face in the boy's shoulder. I could see that she was sobbing.'

'You could only *see* that she was sobbing,' the inspector pointed out. 'Continue.'

'Well, she had just seen her own sister jump into the river, it would have been insensitive—'

'How did you conclude she saw her sister jump? Because the boy told you so? Did he witness the event?'

His subordinate shifted in his chair again, this time uncomfortably. 'No, he isn't a witness.'

'That means no one else can confirm the suicide theory. No witnesses other than the victim's sister Sevita.'

'No, sir, there aren't.'

'I see. Any other detail? What else did you do at the scene?'

'There was a heavy cloud cover over Lavasa this morning, and the river was in spate. We couldn't send the divers on a search mission as it started raining again soon after the incident. No helicopters could take off due to the strong winds. In short, due to adverse weather conditions, we couldn't begin the search till after noon,' Gadre finished. He put a stack of papers on the table. 'We were then able to assign certain areas to search parties after monitoring the flow of the river, but there's no news as of now. Nothing to report yet. In fact, under the present circumstances, it may be impossible to retrieve the body.'

'The body? So you conclude that she is dead?'

'No one could have survived it, sir,' the sub-inspector said. He was taken aback by the inspector's question. Was this what two decades in the crime bureau did to a man? 'The river was flooded; it was flowing very fast. The riverbed is rocky. One can assume she was hit by rocks when she fell and was carried downstream by the currents.'

Mohite scanned the papers his subordinate had placed before him. There were names of possible search locations and members of the designated search parties, forensic reports from the scene and statements from people who were in the vicinity of Lavasa bridge around the time the incident took place. But there was nothing to go on, not a single clue.

'Hmm ... put it all on record. As for the girl, I will take her statement myself. You guys are too soft.'

He flipped a sheet of paper, his eyes moving from left to right rapidly. 'Forensics cannot find a damn clue after all that rain. No blood, no nothing.' Mohite took a deep breath and sat back. 'Who in the area could have seen something, *anything* ...? Who is this Dipesh Pansare?' He held another sheet of paper up in front of them.

'He works as a toll collector on the bridge,' Vikrant said.

'Oh yes, you asked him some questions, right? Tell us.'

'The toll collector's duty had begun at 7 a.m. With zero tourists coming in, there was hardly any traffic. Only a few cars and supply trucks had driven in and out. Dipesh was making himself a cup of tea when he saw two girls standing on the bridge, talking. There is a spare room in one of the buildings next to the bridge, an old post. His kitchen has a window with a direct view of the bridge. He was clearly passing time there.'

'I'm ready to overlook that for now. What else?' The inspector's eyes narrowed as he listened intently.

'He saw them standing there, talking. One of them was leaning on the railing, and the other stood about a metre away, facing her. That was when he was boiling his tea. In another ten seconds or so, he went to fetch a cup and came back to see only one girl still on the bridge. She was staring at the river. The other, the one who had leaned against the railing, was gone.'

'That's it? He didn't hear a scream ... any sound at all?'

'Nothing. He just saw the girl make a call on her phone. Then she sat on her scooter by the roadside for a while, before she left on it. He couldn't describe the clothes or face, and cannot identify her for sure. But they were the only girls on the bridge this morning as per him.'

'He didn't bother to find out what had happened?'

'I don't think so. I doubt he even realized something was wrong.'

'Hmm ... no scream, no call for help ...'

Gadre's eyes narrowed too. He had never come across a case like this where a witness hadn't screamed. In some cases, witnesses fainted from the shock.

Inspector Mohite didn't like the sound of it at all.

'We are missing something,' he declared. 'Bring them all here to record the statements. I want the toll collector first.'

'Yes, sir,' the two men said in unison.

---

'Do you even realize that my daughter died some twenty-five hours ago?' Mr Vyas raged at Vikrant Singh who stood at their door along with another policeman. The police vehicle was parked outside the Vyas home.

'I do, sir. That is why we are here. This is a crucial process. We need Sevita to come along with us.' Vikrant had learnt to mimic Inspector Mohite's hawk-eyed look. That made his interrogations more effective for some reason.

But Mr Vyas was boiling in fury and disgust. He wanted outsiders, the police included, to stay away from his family and allow them to grieve.

'I refuse. Relatives and friends are on their way to our home right now. It is my daughter's funeral.' His voice shook, and his eyes turned red. 'We don't even have her body to cremate. Why don't you work on finding her first?'

'The search parties are already at work, sir. But we need you to cooperate. We understand that this is a tough time, but it's important that the investigation be allowed to continue,' Vikrant said.

The young policeman held up a copy of the day's local newspaper. Mr Vyas's eyes immediately fell on the lead article.

**College Student Jumps to Her Death**

> On the morning of 18 June at around 7.30 a.m., Sama Vyas, a first-year engineering student, died by jumping off the Lavasa bridge. Sama, only seventeen, had just begun college. The tragic act was witnessed by her twin sister, who was with her on the bridge when she took the fatal plunge. The duo were on their way to college.
>
> It is believed that Sama had some social issues. Sources confirm that she was quiet and withdrawn throughout her school years.
>
> This regrettable event also raises questions regarding the safety of the bridge. Is Lavasa bridge safe anymore? Is the railing adequate to prevent a tragic, impulsive decision? Nowadays, we see more and more youngsters succumb to depression, unable to cope with the stress and pressures of—

'Take this out of my sight!' Mr Vyas flailed his arms, striking at the newspaper in agitation. Its pages were scattered on the doorstep. 'Social issues!' he raged, '*Social issues* ... who said that?'

Then his shoulders dropped, and tears filled his eyes.

'Mohan? Are you alright?' Mrs Vyas couldn't bear to see her husband in such a sorry state. 'Please wait,' she said sternly to the policemen and took her husband inside. 'Social issues?' he was hissing in disgust. 'What social issues? Who the hell said that? How can they write this bullshit?'

Sama was watching the whole scene from the corridor. Her mother was whispering to Mr Vyas, and he was nodding, looking resigned. With a sigh, Mrs Vyas eventually turned to look at her daughter, her eyes saying, 'We don't have a choice.'

Sama clenched her palms. She had made the mistake of believing there wouldn't be anything more to worry about. Now she knew she would have to go through the investigation and that she couldn't afford to slip up. Not even once. The only way to do it was to let go of her own identity. Every last bit of it.

How would Sevita act? How would she talk? How would she look?

*That is easy. I can do that part. And if something else happens ... I know I can handle that too.*

She gave her mom a sad smile and nodded, biting her lip. 'Maa, please stay with dad; I will be okay. Promise.'

# VOICES IN THE HEAD

Lavasa's was a small-town police station. The local police and civilians were mostly concerned with trivial problems. The suicide case was extraordinary. Sama could feel people stare at her as she walked in.

A small man came out of the inspector's cabin. He was tiny and shabby, wearing an old white cotton shirt and greyish pants that were too loose for him. Sama knew instantly that she had seen him before. Who was he? Where had she seen him? She just couldn't place him. He looked pale and scared. Could he be a witness?

'Please go in.' Gadre ushered Sama into the cabin. There sat the tall, broad-shouldered man who had asked her those piercing questions the previous day, impeccable in his well-fitting khaki uniform. Now that she saw him closely, she sensed that he was formidable, and it wasn't just his build. His eyes could bore deep into you. And she hated it.

'Please sit down,' said Mohite, his voice crisp and demanding. Sama took the chair in front of him. Vikrant pushed a button on a recording device placed in front of her, without any warning, let alone a request for permission. He also had a notepad with him. Gadre also sat down, across the table from her.

*I am surrounded*, Sama thought. Her mind was getting cloudy, noisy.

'Please state your name for the record,' Mohite said curtly.

She parted her lips that were shut tight. After a second, she said, 'Sevita Vyas.'

'How old are you?'

'Seventeen. '

'What was your relationship with your sister like?'

'I loved her ... but Sama was different ...'

'Explain that in detail.' Mohite's forehead creased. Sama looked into his eyes which seemed to be scrutinizing her. Her mind was still hazy, but this was no time to let the voices take over. They needed to fade out.

'She never reciprocated my feelings; she got irritated when others sympathized with her. Sama was quiet, always in her own world. Sometimes she would go out in the woods to collect moths. It was her hobby ... nothing else really interested her.'

'Insect collection is a hobby that many people pursue. Why do you say it as if it's something out of the ordinary?'

'I didn't find it strange. But Mom didn't like it. She was always harsh on her. She never understood that she was different. Dad wasn't like that; in fact, he got her a new set of tools to catch insects.'

'And you?'

'Me? Her moths never bothered me.' She shrugged slightly, letting her face melt with emotions. 'If she had been with us longer, I would probably have gone out moth-catching with her one day. But some things are not meant to be ...'

'How would you describe yourself?'

'I love to hang out with my friends, go shopping. I think I'm more outgoing.'

'Did you tell her that you approved of her strange hobby?'

'As I said, I never thought it was a strange hobby, just rare ... and no, I didn't have a chance to tell her that. There were other things bothering her that I wanted to talk to her about.' Sama looked down at her hands sadly as she delivered her lines.

'Like what?' Mohite leaned forward.

'Like Nikhil and his gang members from our class always trying to bully her, calling her names, and making hurtful remarks.' There was a shade of anger in her voice.

'Can you give us an example of such a remark?'

'Well, on the very first day of college, they made fun of her name. Sevita means "the one who is cherished". They said Sama must mean "darkness", just because she was an introvert. He didn't put it nicely at all. He compared her to me and called her weird in front of everyone.'

A tear bulged near the corner of her eye.

'It must have been hard for her. You also mentioned that she shut herself inside her room for two days.'

'Yes ... not too long ago, Nikhil bullied her again. Kunal stopped them from doing any harm, but she was ... affected. She just sat in a corner of her room and didn't move at all, though we tried our best.'

'How do you know that?'

'Know what?'

'That she sat in a corner of her room?'

Sama felt a tremor travel up her spine. Mohite's eyes watched her like a hawk's.

'She would always go sit in a corner when she felt bad as a child, so I assume she did the same this time,' she retorted.

*You need to control your anger. Calm down. Be sad and cry.*

'I see. What did you do to try and get her out?'

'I called her phone, knocked on her door and windows, tried speaking to her from outside. But she wouldn't budge. She asked me to go away, leave her alone. Then yesterday, she came out in the morning, dressed for college.'

'What was your reaction?'

'I was happy and asked her to come with me to college. It was a chance to talk to her about her feelings and about her being bullied.'

'What do you mean, go with you to college? Did you go separately on other days?'

'Yes, I always wanted her to ride with me on my scooty, but she didn't like being surrounded by people. I hang out with my friends every day. We start our day at the campus parking lot with a cup of tea. And she didn't like to mingle. So, she started taking the college bus.'

'That doesn't make sense. You could still have gone together. If she didn't like being around your friends, couldn't she simply walk away after reaching college?'

'I did suggest it, but she refused.' Sama could feel her jaws tighten in anger. The man was asking too many useless questions. 'It was her choice. I couldn't interfere.'

'Oh, but I thought you cared,' he said, propping his pointed chin on his knuckles.

'You do not understand. She didn't like to be forced into anything or to be questioned about her decisions.' The voices were hissing angrily in her head. She clutched her skirt under the table.

'I see. So, what happened next? You persuaded her to go with you that day ...'

'Then we rode down the hill and on to the bridge. I wanted a chance to talk to her, but in the open, where she couldn't hide. So I stopped at the bridge.'

'What did you talk about?'

'I asked her what I could do to make things better for her. I told her that we are one as much as we are different. I told her that I loved her and that I would do anything for her. She was my twin sister ...' The tears in the corners of her eyes bulged again, and, this time, they rolled down. She sobbed.

'She said that she believed me and that she wanted to start over. I was so relieved. When I turned to look at the skies, I thought it was a new beginning. But she chose to jump into that angry river—' Sama choked on her words. She wiped her tears on her sleeve. Gadre looked at her with pity. Vikrant also felt a twinge of guilt. Mohite, however, was not moved.

'You must have been scared, so scared.'

'Yes ...'

'Your sister jumped off, and you couldn't do anything to stop her ...'

'I didn't even notice when she jumped off—'

'Then how did you know she had jumped?'

'I heard a splash and looked down at the river. I couldn't believe what I was seeing ... it took me a while to figure out it was her. I was so scared. It was like a nightmare.'

'How long did it take for you to figure it out?' He was eyeing her observantly. She looked at him, feeling annoyed. It was a weird question, and she loathed his face.

'I didn't really check the time ... It took as long as it would take to freeze a heart, I suppose. Seconds? Perhaps minutes?' she said curtly.

'What was your reaction when you figured it out?' he asked calmly, ignoring her sarcasm.

'I didn't know what to do, so I called Kunal on my phone. He said he would be there soon and I should just wait.'

'So let me clarify this,' Mohite tapped the table, leaning towards her with a gaze that sent chills down her spine.

'You heard a splash, looked down and took some moments to figure out what had happened. All this while, where exactly were you standing on the bridge?'

'Near the railing.'

'Was the railing cold?'

'I don't remember. Must've been a bit cold.'

Silence fell. They looked at each other as if blocking the other from reading their thoughts.

'Were you holding the railing?' the inspector continued.

'I don't remember. Maybe at one point.'

'So where were you standing?'

'As I said, I was by the railing. I was looking up at the clouds drifting away. When I heard the splash, I looked down. There ... I saw her surface and float away with the waves.'

'And what was your reaction?'

'I froze. I didn't know what to do. I couldn't jump in after her; the river was fierce.'

'Did you cry out, call for help?'

'There was no one around. I called Kunal.'

'And you sat there waiting for him? Didn't it occur to you to call for help, approach someone who was nearby?'

'I saw no one around. And how would anyone help? It's not like they could have jumped in the river and saved her. Besides, she was already unconscious, ... maybe even dead.'

'How can you say that?' Mohite's eyes were ablaze.

'Because she was not struggling. Even if she jumped, drowning can't be painless. She was not struggling.'

'You didn't stay there, though. You rushed home all of a sudden.'

'It was too painful to wait. I was scared, and I needed my mom. Aren't you done with this pointless interview?'

'I will decide if it is a pointless interview or not. You will answer my questions and as many times as I ask,' Inspector Mohite said in a clear, firm tone.

A burning sensation filled her stomach. She wanted to get out of that office and away from that man.

'What else do you want to know, then?'

'What was the distance between you and the railing of the bridge? Give me an estimate. Stand as far from this table as you were from the railing.'

Sama instantly knew something was wrong. Did someone see them yesterday? Gritting her teeth, she stood up. He was watching her closely. She took a step back. Another, and then one more, walking backwards.

'Hmm ... around a metre.' Mohite pushed himself back against his chair, observing her keenly. Those soft expressions, melting with emotion, were all but gone from her face. Her tears had dried up.

'I guess that's it for now. I have your statement on record and will ask you to come by if need be. I suggest you comply and help in the investigation.'

'Sure, I will do all that I can,' she replied coldly.

Gadre escorted Sama out of the station to a police vehicle.

'What did you think, sir?' Vikrant watched Inspector Mohite ponder over the interrogation he had just concluded, wide-eyed.

'What did you think?' Mohite countered.

'I think there are irregularities. What the toll man saw and what she said matches, but something sounds off.'

'Yes. If she was one metre away from the railing, she should have seen her sister jump off, at least from the corner of her eye. They were not standing that far apart or outside each other's line of sight. How come she didn't notice? She could even have held her back,' he said. 'We are not done here.'

---

Sama's funeral was a short ceremony. There was grief and shock amongst the family and friends who attended. There were also reporters trying to get their news bite, hounding anyone they could find who was related to the case for a juicy titbit.

Mr Vyas's driver, along with some of his work colleagues, took it upon themselves to ensure that he was able to grieve in peace. They helped to keep unwanted people at bay. Kunal, Astha and Shruti made sure that Sevita was never alone; at least one of them was always with her. And how could they leave? She was too vulnerable.

*Are you leaving? Are you going home? Will you be back?* She would ask these questions whenever one of them walked even a few steps away from her. It wasn't easy for them, but it was so much more intense for her, they felt.

A framed photograph was placed on a wall in the main hall. The tragic Monday of the incident seemed to go on and on until the weekend arrived, and all the visiting mourners left. The reporters, tired of waiting for a substantial scoop, had also thinned in numbers.

The following Monday dawned with thick black clouds clustering in Lavasa's sky, like the claw of a predator slowly closing in on its prey.

Sama was in Sevita's bedroom. Mrs Vyas was in the kitchen making breakfast. Mr Vyas had secluded himself in his room. Sama watched the sky get murkier, sitting by the huge window in her sister's room. She raised one knee and clasped her hands around it, placing her cheek on the glass pane. A smile spread on her face. It turned into a little laugh. Something like an ecstatic current ran through her body.

She sprang up and leaped towards the wardrobe. Everything inside it was new. Each piece of cloth would wrap her in a new life. She tried them all on, one by one, and gazed at herself in the mirror attached to the wardrobe door.

'Hi, I'm Sevita! Nice to meet you. Hi, I'm Sevita! So good to see you!' She practised introducing herself with the smile that she had perfected. Although she knew she would have to keep the sad act up a little longer, nothing could stop her from living her new life now.

It was almost time for her to leave for college. She changed into a pair of jeans and an ordinary tee, careful not to put on a lot of makeup and to let her hair be messy. The moment she picked up the scooty's keys, her phone rang.

'Good morning,' Kunal said, trying to sound cheerful.

'Hi,' Sama replied softly. Her heart started to race.

'I'm coming to pick you up. Be outside in five, okay?'

'Okay ...'

She walked out of her room. Mrs Vyas was busy in the kitchen.

'Mom, I'm leaving!' she called out, for the first time in her life, to her mother.

'Okay, sweetie.' Mrs Vyas rushed out with a lunchbox. 'Take care of yourself, okay?' she said and hugged her tightly. Sama felt numb the whole time.

'Yeah, see you,' she mumbled and left, without looking into her mother's eyes. It was a strange feeling to be touched by her mother with affection.

'Sevita!' Kunal called out to her the moment she stepped outside. He was parked a little further down the road. She walked quickly towards him and got into his car.

'How are you?' he asked, watching her worriedly.

'I missed you,' she said softly.

'I'm here now.' He smiled and leaned over to kiss her. She felt dazed when his lips touched hers. He caressed her face with a warm smile and started the car. 'Let's go.'

College seemed so different. A week ago, no one would even have noticed her. Today, all eyes were on her, and none of them held contempt or caution. They were full of sympathy, wonder and concern. Kunal walked with her across the parking lot and to the classroom. Many people came up to her and offered their condolences. They patted her, hugged her, and expressed their support with warm words.

Sama's whole world had turned around. She was excited. Classes began with Prof. Rawat taking attendance. He skipped Sama's name conscientiously. Midway through roll call, Nik and his gang entered the class.

'You haven't taken permission to enter, Nikhil.'

'Sorry, sir, didn't want to disturb you.'

'Why are you late?'

'Morning practice for the race tomorrow. My 001 is gonna win big,' he replied, an overconfident grin cracking open his jaw. The professor was not happy with Nik's behaviour, but he knew that an argument would tip the delicate balance in the class that morning. The mood was already heavy with one empty seat in the back corner. He gestured at him to sit and continued the roll call.

Sama watched him walk towards his seat. Nik had the same smirk on his face that he always did while bullying her. His cronies followed him, looking slightly uncomfortable.

Nik, however, was not affected at all. The very sight of his face made her clench her jaws.

'Don't look at that bastard,' Kunal whispered softly in her ear. He was sitting right behind her. She nodded and looked away, but a voice in her head murmured something in a guttural rumble. What was it saying? She couldn't hear it clearly.

At lunchtime, Astha came and took her hand. 'Hey, come, I've got you some strawberry tarts,' she said. Shruti joined them, a hesitant smile on her face.

The canteen looked alien to Sama; she had never been there. She wanted to eat lunch on her tree stump up in the woods, but today her new surroundings seemed enticing too. Astha and Shruti talked to her about every topic they could find—what she had missed at college the previous week, a boy's failed attempt at asking Astha out, Shruti's flirtatious chats with her latest love interest, a college fest that was coming up ...

'How did everyone react?' Sama asked all of a sudden. Silence fell amongst them.

'Sevita, let's not think about it.' Astha took her hand.

'Was Nik sad even for a second?' she asked bitterly.

Shruti stopped sipping on her buttermilk and looked at Kunal.

'Why do you care about what he thinks?' he tried to make her drop the subject.

'It matters to me. She was my sister. He doesn't care, does he?'

'Even if he does, he would never let it show. That would destroy his sadistic image,' Kunal reasoned.

'So he feels no remorse,' Sama said darkly.

'Sevita,' Kunal said as he leaned close and looked into her eyes. 'I'm telling you not to think of that bastard. Let karma give him what he deserves. Don't waste your thoughts on him, okay? Let's finish lunch and get back to the class.'

Sama nodded.

---

*He will get what he deserves ...* The guttural voice in her head had found the words.

That evening, after Kunal had dropped her off, she took her scooty and rode to the boat club by the river. It was eight o'clock on a dark monsoon night. The boat race contestants had finished their final practice and checked their boats into the assigned slots. The race was to start at seven the next morning.

Sama walked in the shadows and slipped into the club unnoticed. The guards were busy locking the rooms and the shower area; their nightly patrol inside the club was done. The lights went off one by one as the last guard to exit the premises switched them off after checking that the doors were properly shut. She stood silently in a dark corner of the reception area until he was gone.

The water rippled gently in the boathouse, black as ink. She walked down the narrow path leading to the boats. In the very first slot, she saw a boat with '001' printed across its side in black and yellow. It was bobbing up and down gently.

Sama carried a small toolkit that she had brought in her scooty's back box. It was easy to open up the boat's engine and find the right wire. She knew which one was for the brakes. Loosening it took no time at all.

Sama rode away as quickly as possible. She needed to get back before Kunal came over for his nightly visits. She made it minutes before his arrival.

'You are sweating,' he said and held her face in his hands.

'I don't feel well.' She hugged him tightly. Kunal hugged her back. A hot shiver ran down her body. He was irresistible when he held her so close.

'Have you taken any meds?'

'No, I'll be fine.'

They lay down together, holding each other. She listened to him tell her about his day. Hours flew by as they talked. It was all so new, so good.

'I sometimes wonder ... where did she float off to? They still haven't found her,' Sama said. It was almost one o'clock in the night.

Kunal was drowsy, but he replied. 'It seems they may not find her. It has been far too long. We need to accept the fact,' he mumbled, half-asleep.

---

The police investigation of Sama Vyas's death, led by Inspector Mohite, was turning out to be more exhausting by the day. His subordinates had started showing signs of hopelessness.

'Why is he so stuck on finding the body? What will he even find now?'

'The girl must have become fish poo by now. There is no sense in continuing the search anymore. It has been ten days.'

Some junior officers had even begun questioning his orders.

'Sir, you shouldn't be interviewing the girl again. She has already been interviewed twice. The parents have gone through two rounds of questioning too. What else do you hope to find?' Gadre had finally found his voice.

Mohite was livid, but he had to agree. He couldn't keep questioning the same people over and over again. However, there was one more person he wanted to question.

So, early in the morning on day eleven of the investigation, instead of going to his station, he drove to the Lavasa Boat Club.

He chose a spot to stand in the open parking lot, away from the people who had gathered to watch the race. He leaned against the wall and lit a Cuban cigar held between his teeth. He could watch all the cars enter from his position. It was a clear, sunny day. Midway through his cigar, a black car turned dangerously fast into the parking lot, leaving the imprint of its tyres on the concrete ground. Mohite walked towards it.

'I could fine you for reckless driving, you know,' he said, as the driver got out of the car.

'And I can see you smoking here on the club premises. That's worth a complaint, right?' Nik said impudently, slamming his car door shut and glaring at the man in front of him.

'I don't see a "no smoking" sign here. But I do see a "drive below 20 kmph" sign. So you're guilty as charged.' Mohite grinned in amusement.

'Who the fuck are you?' Nik retorted, moving closer to the man as he glared at him.

'Inspector Mohite. I'm in charge of Sama's suicide case. Need to ask you a few questions.'

Nik's anger evaporated as he retreated a step or two from the tall, imposing man. 'Look, it's 6 a.m. already. I have to take part in a race at seven. What do you want?' He tried to sound tough.

'Answers.'

'What kind of answers?'

'I will be the one asking the questions. And I want straightforward answers.'

'You don't have the right—'

'I could get an arrest warrant for you if you want. After all, you are the one who bullied Sama and are the only suspect in this case so far.'

Nik gulped. Beads of sweat appeared on his forehead.

'I have your attention now, I see.' Mohite took another puff.

'Fine, ask away. But I have nothing to do with whatever happened to that girl.'

'Such indifference ... any reason you hated her so much?'

'She never stood up for herself. I hate people who let others bully them. Her weirdness was irritating.'

'So, is it justifiable to bully those who are weird?'

'She was not disadvantaged in any way. I wouldn't bully a disabled person. People said she had social issues, but I think not. That girl was smart; she got top grades without attending many classes. I knew her since high school. I believe she was hiding something.'

'Why do you say she was hiding something?'

'I just know.' Nik closed his eyes as he tried to put his thoughts into words. 'Every time I said something to her, I'm sure she had a retort in mind, but she never voiced it. She was smart enough to know how to avoid us. That means she knew where we were all the time, our routines, and exactly how to sneak away unnoticed.'

'Isn't that necessary to escape a bully?'

'Yeah, that's what I thought. Except for that last time,' he said. A nerve under his eye twitched.

'What happened?'

'See, I know I was a bit out of line.' He let out a small sigh. 'But I was never going to hurt her. She was sitting alone on a tree stump. She thought no one would find her in that place, but I followed her one day. I had decided to make her say something, force her to resist, so I threatened her ... not physically or anything ... just a little act. I walked towards her and ... something was strange about that girl, I swear.'

'What was strange?' Mohite pressed on.

Nik shifted on his feet, becoming even paler, his breathing raspy. 'I saw it in her eyes. The moment I was about to step within arm's reach, it was as if she was about to kill me.'

'You mean it was anger?'

'No,' Nik snorted. 'It wasn't just that. It was cold, unfeeling. Like when a snake bites. I know it sounds weird, but there was nothing like fear or anger in those eyes.' He shook his head.

'What did you do?'

'I stopped right in my tracks. Just then, Kunal came at me with a crazy punch and knocked me down ... asshole.'

'How would you describe Sama, other than as a weird girl with a cold stare who never responded to your jibes?'

'Withdrawn. She never spoke to anyone except Kunal. I'd never even seen her talk to her own sister, and I've known these two girls for a couple of years now. She had a knack of becoming invisible in a crowd. People usually didn't notice her.'

'Why did you notice her?'

'Me? Well, I guess I was similar to that girl. In middle

school, I was skinny and tiny. People never spoke to me,' Nik spoke haltingly.

'They made fun of you, and you never retaliated either, because you were afraid?'

'Yeah … I was scared.'

'That's why she irritated you?'

'Right. But she wasn't scared. I know that much now,' he said. 'I was similar maybe, but not the same.'

'I see. No one ever is the same as another person.'

'Yeah, I mean, those twins are the best example. Sevita is completely the opposite of her sister. She loves to talk, makes friends easily, gets emotional and dramatic. She is totally different. Not since Sama's suicide, though; she's too depressed.'

'Who can blame her?'

'You can't …' Nik let out a deep breath. 'See, sir, I never imagined she would take a step like that. Maybe, I read her wrong. Maybe, things went out of hand for her … I can't say why she did it. I'm not thrilled about it.'

'Are you remorseful?'

'Why should I be remorseful?'

'It is human nature to feel bad about such events.'

'I told you I am not thrilled. Count that as being sad, if you want.' Nik shrugged.

'Hmm … right. I will talk to you again if need be,' Mohite said as he looked at him keenly. He could see that his pupils did not constrict. He wasn't blinking too much either. The boy was unaffected by his questioning.

'Sure.' Nik nodded and turned to leave.

'Before you go, how much did you make by telling the reporters about Sama's social issues?'

Nik froze in his tracks before he turned around.

'Ten thousand. I needed a new life-vest for my boat race. Are you going to call me a criminal for that?'

'Nah, they would have got the information they wanted sooner or later. See you around, kid.'

---

Mohite walked away, puffing the remainder of his cigar and thinking. This case was like trying to hold cigar smoke in his palms. Or was there something concrete that he couldn't grasp yet?

There was no body, no forensic evidence, no real witness except Sevita. What Nik told him gave him an insight into Sama's personality, but not much more. If only they had found the body, in whatever shape, some clue could have been recovered, but that was unlikely now. He stood in the parking lot, smoking.

'Gadre,' he made a call to the sub-inspector, 'call off the search. I want everyone back at the station. I'll join you a little later today.'

The wind was picking up speed. Mohite watched a large college crowd gather, shouting in excitement and hoisting banners. He put his cigar out and followed the crowd towards a barricaded road facing the river. Volunteers were posted to divert vehicles from entering the area to ensure the safety of the spectators. Noise and energy levels were high.

Mohite stood in a corner and took out another cigar. Anyone looking at the serene river that morning would laugh at the thought of someone jumping in its waters to end their life. The contestants were ready in their speed boats at the edge of the river. They were giving their machines a final check. He saw Nik inspect the boat's engine and put on his life-vest and helmet with care.

'Are we ready to go?' A girl's voice blared through a hand-held loudspeaker. The crowd cheered, as the contestants took their positions with thumbs-up gestures. Engines roared to life. The announcer had introduced the contestants and their boats to the crowd, raising the energy, and was waving a flag that would signal the start.

'So here we go! Ready ... set ... GO!'

The racers shot forward on their boats like bullets. In no time, Nik and contestant number 005 were vying for the lead. It was a short race, so the right kind of manoeuvring was crucial. Nik was behind by a fraction of a second. He sensed that his only chance at victory was boosting his speed in the final seconds. It was a risky move, but he was confident that he would pull it off. The trophy would be his!

As they neared the finish line, Nik increased his speed a notch. Contestant 005 was now in second place. Nik was exhilarated. He knew he would win this race, and he was right. There was a strong wind behind him, and he realized he needed to brake the moment he crossed the finish line. Within a second of his crossing the line, he eased on the speed and pushed the brake.

Something was wrong. The boat wasn't stopping. He was supposed to stop well before the bridge pillars. He zoomed ahead at high speed. The wind was lashing at his back. Nik couldn't understand what was happening. He lost balance, and his boat rammed straight into one of the pillars that supported Lavasa bridge. He fell off the boat, and his head struck the pillar.

The crowd was shocked into silence. Contestant number 005 dived into the water, along with the guards in the judge's boat. Mohite rushed into the club. He instructed the doctors on stand-by in a boat to rush to the spot.

Contestant 005 managed to pull Nik out of the water.

He was taken ashore where an ambulance was waiting. A medic attempted CPR as they rushed him to the hospital. But the impact with the pillar had shattered his neck. Bones had torn his windpipe. Nik never came back despite the doctor's best efforts. He was declared dead thirty minutes after the accident.

The second death within a fortnight shocked the town into silence.

—

'I am having very strange thoughts. I don't know what to do,' Sama said as she clung to Kunal that evening when he dropped her off from college. 'I used to curse Nik and look what happened. Is this my fault?' She covered her face in dismay.

'No, Sevita, look at me.' He took her hands into his. 'You had nothing to do with this. It was an accident. Everyone knows that, right? He was going too fast, it was windy, he lost his balance.'

'Hmm... I don't want to be alone tonight.' She looked at him tenderly.

'Hey ...' He pulled her closer into a tight hug. 'It's just a matter of a few hours. You know I will be back, right?' He combed her hair with his fingers. She nodded.

As promised, a few hours later, Kunal made his way inside her room through the window. All night Sama clung to him, not letting him move one step away from her. Kunal let her rest on his chest and sleep.

The fatigue of constantly caring for her was tiring Kunal out. *I have to be with her at least for a few more days till she heals*, he thought as she peacefully slept in his arms.

# THE PUPPETEER

Another week passed by. Nik's tragic death was still the talk of the town. Kunal felt suffocated. Wherever he went, people spoke about unpleasant things. He had stopped going out with his football buddies to avoid discussions about sad topics or being asked about Sevita and how she was doing. That day, he skipped football and went straight to class. Sama had gone to the canteen for a cup of coffee. Kunal wanted a breather. He wanted to be alone for just a few minutes. He silently sat inside the classroom.

A boy entered the classroom just then.

'Sup Nitin,' Kunal greeted him as he put his bag on his desk.

'All good. You tell me.'

'Cool.' He shrugged in response, hoping to curb more conversation.

'You know, Kunal,' Nitin said, 'there's this college fest in Pune day after tomorrow. I'm going with a few of my friends.'

'Oh, great.'

'Why don't you join us?'

'I … I don't know, man. I don't want to leave Sevita alone.'

'Bring her along. It will do us all good if we get out of here for a bit.'

It wasn't a bad idea. Probably a change of atmosphere would be good for Sevita and him. The idea of getting out for some time, simply escaping, was enticing.

---

On Friday afternoon, Kunal, Sama, Shruti and Astha, together with another boy from their class, set off for the fest. They followed Nitin's Mercedes GLS, which was loaded with six people.

'I never knew he had a Merc. What is he even doing in this town?' Kunal's friend was in high spirits, mesmerized by Nitin's shining black car. Sama, meanwhile, was not happy to have to sit in the back seat. Shruti and Astha clicked selfies, asking her to pout or at least smile. It was a beautiful cloudy day, with bursts of sunshine as they drove along a smooth road.

'Just pray it doesn't rain, or we will have to stay over in Pune,' Kunal said, glancing at the clouds. He already felt more free. It was relaxing to roll the windows down and feel the pleasant breeze.

They arrived at the grounds where the 2020 youth fest 'Sparkle' was taking place. It was an enormous gathering with students from all over the state. The whole affair was managed by college students. Laughter and chatter kept the place abuzz.

Kunal parked his car beside Nitin's, and the group got out, stretching their limbs after the long drive. It was almost four in the evening. They first stopped at a café stall for refreshments. After that, they split into smaller groups to look for stalls set up by entrepreneurs and companies of their interest. Kunal found a stall set up by a documentary filmmaking company. They were offering an internship programme in Assam. Sama was with him. Shruti joined them too, standing next to Kunal. Sama stood silently, watching Shruti and measuring the distance between her and Kunal.

'Isn't this an amazing opportunity for you?' Shruti asked Kunal. 'You have always wanted to shoot in scenic places.' She was just an inch away from touching him.

'Yes, but I can't skip a semester, so it's a no-go. I can find something else,' he replied. Sama stayed silent.

Next, they went to a café. Kunal ordered a double chocolate milkshake.

'Make it two,' Shruti said, smiling widely.

'No, three,' Sama said. Her gaze was pinned on Shruti's face. The way she walked when Kunal was close, the way she tossed her hair whenever he turned to her, the way she looked at him ... Sama felt the hair on the back of her neck bristle. She remembered the day they had gone to a movie together. It had been the same that day too. Shruti had been watching Sevita and Kunal all the time, looking away whenever they moved closer to each other or held hands. Sama knew that Sevita had known about Shruti's feelings for Kunal but had chosen to let it go.

*Sadly for her, I'm not that stupid.*

---

By the time the sun set, the ground was lit up with bulbs and fairy lights. Stages were set up, like at a fair, where people danced, sang, played music and performed skits.

'What do you want to see first?' Kunal asked Sama, smiling happily for the first time in weeks.

'Oh look, there's a puppet show,' Sama said, pointing behind him.

'A puppet show?' Kunal had never seen her show interest in a puppet show. He chuckled at her whim, however, and walked towards the puppet show with her. Shruti was still tagging along. Astha had disappeared a while ago, saying she had to meet a friend. Sama knew who that friend was.

They approached the stage, with Shruti close behind them and found an empty bench. Clouds were starting to gather above them. Kunal looked up apprehensively, his smile fading away.

'I think we should head back soon,' he said. 'Seems like it can rain anytime.'

'After this, show, please?' Sama said, not wanting to miss it.

'What's so great about this? You never even liked such things,' Kunal asked, irritated. He was scared of getting caught in the rain.

'I like puppets. Someone is manipulating them on strings, but you can't see it. That is such an art,' she said adamantly. Shruti was looking at both of them in confusion. Kunal couldn't put a finger on what was getting on his nerves. Was it the tone of her voice or her stubbornness?

'Fine. I'll wait in the car.' He stood up and walked off.

'Umm … I'll get something to eat and maybe see you later in the car?' Shruti also stood up.

'You really want to get something to eat or is this a ruse to sit in the car alone with Kunal?' Sama's eyes flashed.

'What do you mean?' Shruti reddened.

'You know very well what I mean. You think I'm blind?' Sama raised a brow.

'Sevita,' Shruti frowned, 'I said I'm going to get something to eat and then I'll go to the car. I can't be with you all the time.'

'Oh, you are not with *me* the whole time. We both know that,' Sama said icily though her insides were starting to burn.

'What do you mean?' Shruti gulped, in a desperate attempt to hide the truth. Sama stood up, glaring at Shruti.

'Kunal loves me,' Sama said in a voice as cold as her glare. 'No one can get in between us. You, of all the women in the world, don't stand a chance.' She said the last words slowly as if to nail them into Shruti's head.

'Yeah? Seeing how you treat him these days, your claim won't hold for much longer,' Shruti retorted, glaring back at her. 'A few more days and he'll be tired of babysitting you, just like we all are.'

'Babysitting me? No, you've found a reason to hang around him all day. It's not me you care about. It never was!'

'At first I did. But you are just sucking our blood, aren't you? You need someone with you all the time! Well, guess what? I'm not up for it. And as far as Kunal is concerned, you always knew I had feelings for him first. Before I could make a move, you stepped in between. Have you forgotten?'

'Turn back time and try. He will fall for me, all over again,' Sama said through gritted teeth. If only Shruti were a moth, she would have pinned her alive on a board.

'I don't know about the past, but let's see how the future goes. See you in the car.'

With that cutting retort, Shruti walked straight to the parking area. Sama watched her for some time before she took her seat. The show was still going on. The puppets were dancing round and round, hanging in the air in their vivid, shimmering costumes.

Sama sat there, unmoving, thinking about what Shruti had just said. What if her words came true? What would she do if she lost Kunal? Her new life would be meaningless.

Though the voices in her head hissed and whispered menacing words, her very core shook in fear. Sama stood up and quietly walked to the parking lot. Shruti was inside the car talking to Kunal. She sat next to him in the front seat. Sama's head felt heavy with a dull ache. She quietly opened the back door and sat inside. Kunal didn't say anything. She could see his eyes in the car's front mirror. He was frowning, glancing repeatedly at the sky and then at his phone.

'Where the hell were you?' he spat at his friend who turned up just then with packets of chips for everyone.

'Chill, dude, I was just getting some snacks,' he said, surprised.

'Astha messaged that she's with some other friends. Let's go.' Kunal strapped his seat belt on, still disgruntled. He drove silently. His friend put some music on to lighten the mood. Shruti looked victorious sitting in the front seat. A few hours later, Kunal dropped Shruti and his friend off. Sama didn't move to the empty front seat, and he didn't ask her to. He drove to Sama's place, parking the car in front of her gate. It was almost midnight. Kunal turned the music off.

'I'll see you tomorrow, then. Really tired,' he said, not looking at her. Sama froze. Was Shruti right?

'Kunal, I'm sorry for today. Please don't be angry,' she said, her voice soft.

'I just need some rest.'

'Will you come in for a little while? I'll make coffee for us,' she pleaded.

Kunal was quiet for a few seconds before he sighed.

'Okay, but I need to leave soon. I'm really tired.'

Sama gave him a well-practised smile.

'The weather is just begging us to have coffee, right?' she said. They were sitting in her room, sharing a mug of coffee.

'Kunal, I know I've been a burden these past two weeks.'

She put her finger on his lips. 'Listen ... I know I have. I want to thank you for taking care of me.'

'Sevita,' he held her hand softly. 'I was just upset because ... well, the weather is really gloomy. It reminds me of that day when Sama ... you know ...' He shifted uncomfortably.

'Yeah? Then let me give you another memory of this weather. A good one.'

'You already have! This coffee tastes gr—'

Before he could say anything else, Sama had leaned over and pressed her lips to his. Her hands moved inside his shirt, feeling his cool skin. The rush of sensations made Kunal loosen up. He wrapped his arms around her waist. Her skin felt hot to his touch, burning through her shirt. He could feel her back curve beneath his hands as she pressed him down on her bed.

'Wait ... Sevita ... you didn't want to do this so soon.' He looked up at her, breathless.

'A lot has changed. I want this. I want you,' she whispered.

She looked into his eyes intently. He caressed her face and pulled her closer to him. The heat was now too much to take. Sama pulled his clothes off and undressed herself. Kunal couldn't believe it was real when he saw her naked for the first time. The beautiful locks of hair touching her slender waist and her skin glowing in the warm light of the lamp were like a dream. She seemed to shimmer in the yellow light.

'You are so beautiful ...' His heart raced, and he rolled her over. 'I love you,' he said as he kissed her lips and neck before moving further down. Sama felt like bursting when his hands reached her breasts. She clutched the sheets, moaning, as he moved over her. He gripped her tighter and kissed her harder, until the pent-up emotions of many years and all his love for her broke out of him.

Sama had never felt so fulfilled. She had never felt so wanted. The voices didn't disturb her for the first time in her life. At one in the night, Kunal was still cuddling her, groggy with sleep. He had messaged his parents that he would be staying over at his friend's place in Pune as it was very late.

Early next morning, it rained. Sama watched the dim, bluish tint in the sky grow brighter behind the sheath of rain. Kunal was asleep, his arm over her stomach. She listened to his calm breathing. One side of her lip curved into a smile.

*He is mine now. Mine.*

---

The day felt different. Kunal felt light and happy all morning, even in the downpour. On their way to college, he made sure to stop by a tea stall and, when Sama was not looking, picked a few flowers for her. He brought them to her along with a hot cup of tea. She was speechless as she looked at them. They were white with a splash of red in the centre. The beautiful petals were covered with tiny droplets of water.

'Wildflowers. Apt for us, aren't they?' He gazed at her. She smiled and nodded, smelling the flowers. They had a very light fragrance, almost undetectable. She had no liking for flowers or fragrances, but his gesture made her feel special.

After a twenty-minute drive with some of his favourite music playing, they reached college. Kunal found a spot in the middle of the parking area.

'Let's go?' He unbuckled his seat belt. Before he could get out of the car, Sama held his hand, looking intently into his eyes. His heart raced. She looked so freakishly beautiful with those wide, brown eyes. Her skin glowed with a strange sheen, something he had never noticed before. It was as if she wasn't the Sevita he knew. He was spellbound. His voice wouldn't escape his throat, and he couldn't move. She leaned over and gave him a long kiss.

'Now let's go,' she finally said, biting the corner of her lip. Kunal took a long breath as she gracefully stepped out of the car. He had to recalibrate his senses before getting out. They walked towards the college building, hand in hand.

'Oh, I forgot my assignment in the car. Wait here; I'll go get it.' He squeezed Sama's hand and rushed back to the parking lot. She waited near a tree, watching him from a distance. In a few minutes, she could see Kunal running back with an assignment file. Suddenly she spotted Shruti running up to him and tapping him on his shoulder. She had a broad smile on her face. Kunal greeted her, and they started talking. The conversation seemed to take a dramatic turn as Shruti's face became serious all of a sudden. She was rubbing her hands together nervously and looking down at the ground as she spoke, glancing up at him from time to time.

'What do you mean you know I must be tired of all this?' Kunal asked Shruti, frowning slightly.

'It's the way she's been acting. She has become very demanding. All this time, Astha and I felt it must be the shock and grief, but now I am not sure. I always see you with her, supporting her, but it must be really hard for you, Kunal. She was acting quite strange yesterday, too, and I can see how stressed you've been lately. You should take a break from her.'

Kunal chuckled, shaking his head in disbelief.

'Take a break from her for whose benefit? Mine or yours, Shruti?'

'What? I don't know what you are saying,' Shruti said, turning red in the face.

'We both know what I am saying. I'm sorry, but she's the woman I love. It has been the same since high school. I was in love with her from the day I saw her and nothing can change that. Whatever happens, no matter how tough it gets, I won't leave her side. Stop embarrassing yourself,' Kunal told her as politely as he could. He looked at her, as if repulsed by her sight, shook his head once again and walked away. Shruti stood rooted to the spot, numb from head to toe.

'What was she saying?' Sama asked him when he walked up to her. 'She doesn't look so good ...'

'Oh, nothing. She wanted to know if we are planning to go to Nitin's birthday party.'

'Yeah? We are going, I suppose?'

'Of course we are!' He pinched her cheek. She smiled, touching the spot his hand had touched.

*The time has come for that scum to learn*, a voice echoed in Sama's head as they walked to their classroom.

---

The day was dull and grey. Faint sunshine peeked through the clouds. Their classroom was so dark that they had to turn the lights on. Sama's eyes bored into Shruti's back as she watched her. It was as if red ants were biting her arms and torso. She watched Shruti raise her hand to answer every question asked by the professor in class. She watched her as she took notes meticulously. She watched her as, at lunchtime, for the first time ever, Shruti left the classroom before Sama and Kunal. Sama saw her say something to

Astha before they walked out together. Astha had a confused frown on her face.

'I'm famished. Let's run,' Kunal said, stuffing his notebooks inside his desk drawer.

'They aren't joining us?' Sama asked, keeping her tone casual.

'Who cares? I'm so hungry I could eat a dinosaur.' He avoided meeting her eyes. 'Come, I'll treat you today,' he said with a smile and took her hand, leading her outside.

She followed him to the canteen. Kunal was quiet all the way. They sat together at their usual corner table. Astha and Shruti had disappeared.

'What did she say, Kunal?' she asked, once they were done with lunch. Kunal silently sipped his lemonade.

'I told you she was asking about the party,' he said after a pause.

'After that?'

'Can we not discuss this?' he said, a tinge of irritation in his voice.

'She has been acting weird, so I'm concerned, that's all. First the Pune college fest and now this—' She stopped eating and kept her fork down, frowning.

'What happened at the fest?' He had never seen Sevita so upset. She must have noticed Shruti tagging along his side, Kunal fretted.

'She left when you did and told me she'd wait in the car with you. She was rude.'

Kunal sighed. Shruti was clearly being mean to Sevita and trying to make her look bad in front of him.

'Sevita, we'd decided to ignore Shruti's behaviour. Perhaps she's still not over us being together. We just have to let go of it. I love you, and that's a fact.' He leaned towards her, locking his gaze with her fiery eyes, and took her hands. 'No one and nothing can ever pull us apart. Not her or anybody else. I need you to take care of yourself and not worry about others, okay?'

'Okay,' Sama murmured, imitating Sevita's perfect smile. Inside her, however, it was a different story. A tsunami of rage was lashing within. She now had the motive she was looking for.

*She tried to take him away from me. It's time to tame her.*

---

After lunch, Shruti and Astha returned five minutes late to class. Neither of them looked at Sama. Shruti had an overdone expression of innocence on her face when she took her seat. Sama watched her sit in front of her. There was a flicker in her eyes, though, and her head tilted to her right.

'Class, today we'll have a pop quiz,' said their chemistry professor, pushing back her glasses. 'This will be a graded group activity, and you will be in pairs. I will give you ten minutes to revise what we have learnt till now.'

The class groaned collectively as everyone opened their books.

'Listen carefully,' the professor continued, 'the groups will be given points for every correct answer and minus one for every incorrect answer. Pair up according to your roll numbers, please. 1 and 2, 3 and 4 ...'

Students continued to grumble under their breath as they moved around to sit with their respective partners. Shruti sat straight-backed with an air of confidence. She was one of the best students in their batch, and such tests didn't faze her.

'34 and 35,' the professor called out.

Shruti looked at Sevita and gave a curt smile. Sevita was roll number 34, while she was 35. Sevita had never been good at studies, and Shruti often coached her for their exams. Chemistry was one of her weakest subjects.

'I'll handle this, no problem,' Shruti said, brimming with confidence. She expected Sevita to come and sit next to her. Sama didn't move. She continued to stare at Shruti, making her more and more uncomfortable. The professor pressed the quiz timer in her hand. Their time had begun. Shruti realized that she would have to shift or lose her revision time in a staring game.

'I know chemistry is not your strong point, so let me handle this. I can't afford to lose marks in a stupid quiz like this,' she said, sitting down next to Sama while avoiding her disturbing gaze. Sama watched her lips move but heard no words. Heat was slowly spreading in her bloodstream. The minutes ticked away.

'Time's up. Close your books and please keep your phones aside,' the professor said. Shruti sighed and put her notes away. If only she could've had a few more minutes.

'Points will be awarded to the group, not individuals. Bonus points if both members of the team answer. Remember, I'm not going to make it easy.'

The professor cleared her throat and began. 'Look at the first equation written on the board. What equation is it?'

'Schrödinger's equation for hydrogen,' Sama answered before anyone else could even read what was written on the board. Heads turned towards her. Shruti was shocked. She turned to Sama and was met with a bland stare.

'What formula did Planck give us?'

'E=nhv,' Sama answered again before anyone could, her stare so cold now that it nearly froze Shruti in her seat.

'What is the energy required to ionize a hydrogen atom?'

'$2.18 \times 10^{-18}$ joule or 13.6 electron volts,' she answered again. Shruti had the answer on the tip of her tongue, but she couldn't speak. Her skin was tingling with fear.

'What is the energy required to excite 1 mole of hydrogen atoms from n=2 state to n=7 state? Let someone else answer, Sevita. You have done very well.' The teacher pointed to another team.

Sama looked at Shruti as if she was insignificant and disgusting. Shruti could feel her hands shake a little. Those eyes were not human. This was not the Sevita she knew. Her heartbeat grew louder.

'It's okay, Shruti, not everyone is good at studies. Perhaps you have some other qualities.' Sama's voice was chilling. Shruti couldn't move even though she wanted to run. What was happening?

Sama's phone vibrated with a message from Kunal:

*That was awesome!*

She smiled, lowering the phone so Shruti could look at the screen, and texted back:

*Thanks! Can't wait to be with you after class. Just you and I, alone ...*

Burning tears filled Shruti's eyes. She stood up and went back to her desk, dropping her pen. A few girls snickered at her clumsiness. She held back her tears and took her seat, rigid as a wooden statue. The moment the class was over, Shruti ran out of the classroom. Astha followed her.

'Madam know-it-all,' Kunal came up to Sama, a huge smile on his face. 'Come for a drive with me?'

'Sure! I'll teach you something you don't know.' She smiled playfully and packed her bag. He was already excited about their date. Nothing else mattered.

Clouds whirled in the sky as they drove up the hills. It started to rain. Kunal turned into a narrow path on a hill;

it was the spot where he had first kissed Sevita. He stopped at a safe distance from the edge. They could see the sliver of the river, grey and dark, from where they parked.

'The weather is rougher than I thought. Maybe we should go—'

'Remember that night when we first came here?' Sama said, leaning over the steering and stopping the windshield wipers of the car. The view in front of them dissolved in the stream pouring over the glass.

'Of course.' He smiled, resting back on his seat to have a better look at her. The white top she wore was almost translucent. Her skin, pale and smooth over her cleavage, made his mouth go dry.

'You remember how scared I was? At the same time, I was so happy.' She inched closer to him. 'You held me, and we kissed,' she said and straddled him. They were face to face now. She smiled and leaned closer. He could feel her breath, while the warm weight of her body on his thighs made his heart race. Her hands trailed over the buttons of his shirt. One by one, she undid them.

'Sevita, it's not ... safe on the hill—'

'Shh ...,' she said and placed a finger on his lips. She could sense how difficult it was for him to resist her. That made it all the more fun!

She took his hands and guided them under her top. Her lips barely touched his as she moved her hips in circles over his lap. Kunal lost all control. His hands moved like she wanted, he kissed her where she wanted, he did what she wanted. Thunder accompanied the singing rain, but all he heard was her heavy breathing. It was only when it was pitch dark outside and the rain had stopped lashing against the car's roof that he became aware of how late it was. They laughed, looking at each other, sweaty and flushed despite the cold rains. That night, even though he was drained, he couldn't help but go back to her.

The next few days went by like a dream. They couldn't keep their hands off each other, even in the campus parking lot or the empty college corridors. They were together all the time.

# MOTHS WITH THEIR WINGS PINNED

Kunal got back home one morning well in time for breakfast. His father was still asleep, but his mother was awake.

'Morning, Maa,' he said, giving her a hug.

'Since you started college, you've forgotten your mother,' she said and pushed him away. 'I'm so angry with you. Why are you never home?' She sounded cross, but her face depicted anxiety. Kunal noticed dark circles around her eyes. Had she been waiting up for him?

'That's not true, Maa.' He cupped her face gently, trying to cheer her up.

'Then why can't you say no to your friends once in a while? I need my son, too.'

The concern in her eyes pierced him sharply.

'I'm sorry. I won't make you worry anymore, I promise.' He hugged her again. 'But this weekend is Nitin's birthday party, remember?'

'Just come back home today.'

'I will,' he said and hugged her. She smiled and patted his back gently.

For weeks, he had completely ignored his family and disregarded their wishes, but the anxiety on his mother's face had shaken him. It was time he set things right.

That day after class, he simply took Sama straight to her house without a word.

'Why are we stopping here? Aren't we going to the hills?'

'Sevita,' Kunal sighed, 'I need a break today. Maa gets worried when I'm out all the time. I need some rest too.' He glanced at her, wondering how she'd react.

'We could just talk ...'

'You know that's impossible. We've tried.'

'I haven't,' she said and looked at him. From the way he looked back, she knew he had made his decision already.

'I'm sorry, I couldn't speak about this earlier today ... it just gets out of hand sometimes,' Kunal said. He had a defiant frown on his face that Sama had never seen before. It was useless to try and persuade him, so she put on a smile.

'I understand, Kunal. If I didn't see you for a day, it would kill me too. You have to take care of her if she's worried.' She leaned over and gently kissed him. 'I'll see you at college tomorrow.'

'Thanks, Sevita.' He caressed her cheek and smiled, mildly surprised.

Sama walked towards her house. She turned to look at him and waved. He waved back and left.

---

Mrs Vyas was excited to see her daughter back early and started talking to her about all sorts of things while setting up lunch. Sama was finding it difficult to be Sevita that day. Her skin burned, and she was too distracted to pretend to listen to her mother.

'I'm tired. I should take a nap,' she said and excused herself. For hours, she sat on her bed, staring at her laptop screen. There was nothing to do, no one to spy on. She opened Sevita's social media accounts and decided to post a picture of herself with a perfect smile. Three hundred likes and fifty comments in a single hour. They did not include Kunal's. He had not seen her picture. Was he drifting away? Did he not want her anymore? He had said he needed to rest...

*He will get tired of you, like we all are*, the voice inside her head repeated Shruti's words. Sama fidgeted. Sevita's room had no jar of insects. There was no way to vent her feelings. It was aggravating.

Her phone rang.

'Hi! Sup? What are you two up to?' It was Nitin. Horns blared in the background.

'I'm at home. Kunal dropped me off.'

'What? We're going to have some pizza. I called you to convince him to join us, because he's unreachable. It would be great to have you, or I'd say even better,' Nitin said with a laugh.

'Oh, sure. Why not? I love pizza.' Anything was better than being left alone in her current state.

'Awesome! I'll come and pick you up. If Kunal picks up his phone, I'll bring him with me.'

'Okay, I'll get ready.'

Sama opened her sister's wardrobe and scanned through the neat piles of dresses, tops and bottoms. Sevita would wear something fresh and catchy, so she chose a pair of denim shorts and a flared red top. She got dressed in a hurry and managed to put some makeup on. Half an hour later, Nitin's Mercedes was waiting for her at the gate. He was standing outside, smoking a cigarette. When she came out, he put it out and smiled, opening the front door of the car for her.

'Sorry, needed a smoke.'

'I don't mind.'

'Kunal is not answering. Is everything okay?'

'Yes, he was just tired today.'

'What are you doing to a man who can play an entire football match without a trip to the bench?' He smiled teasingly.

'You have no idea,' she said and returned the teasing smile.

Nitin brushed his hair back, blushing slightly. 'Anyway, a lot of people are coming, and I hope you have fun. It's my friend's hotel up the hill. He's introducing a new menu,' Nitin said as he revved the car.

---

Many people had gathered to celebrate the launch of the new menu. He introduced her to everyone and involved her in all conversations. People she had never met before talked to her and saved her number. As pizza after pizza was served up, pictures were taken and videos made. She was being tagged in them all. Sama felt special.

She noticed that Kunal hadn't liked a single post. He also hadn't called her back.

So, that night when he did call her, she chose not to answer. The next morning she acted like nothing was wrong.

'Hey, you didn't answer my call last night?'

'You didn't pick up when I called in the afternoon,' she said softly, closing the car door.

'I told you I was tired. I was asleep.' He sounded irked.

'I slept early too. We had gone for pizza, and I was stuffed. It made me so sleepy.'

'Pizza? With whom?' He frowned.

'You didn't check Facebook or Instagram?'

'No. Why are you being like this?'

'Kunal, relax! It was Nitin and some people from his group. We called you many times, but you didn't answer.'

Kunal looked ahead as he drove. He hadn't gone online at all the previous day. He had wanted a break.

Sama let out a calculated sigh. 'Don't get agitated. It's okay if I didn't answer your call, just like it's okay that you didn't. We can't be together all the time, like you said.'

He blinked. Were those words genuine or was she being sarcastic? She wasn't even looking at him. Whatever it was, he thought, he would make it up to her.

---

'Sorry, I'm going boating with some people. Why don't you join us?' Sama said to Kunal after the class. He had wanted to take her out for coffee.

'No, I can't stay late,' he said. He had assumed Sevita would want to spend time with him, especially after last night.

'That's too bad. But I understand. You need to spend more time with your family,' she said softly, lightly touching his chest. She let her gaze linger over his lips before looking up at him.

Kunal wasn't sure what he was feeling. The more he tried not to think about it, the more trapped he felt. His parents had been happy to have him home the previous night. But was he missing out in the bargain? He felt excluded.

A long and excruciating week passed by. Shruti had tried to call him, even talk to him in class about why he was looking troubled. He didn't respond, irritated by her attempts, especially since he knew what her agenda was.

*Tell me what's wrong, Kunal. I'm here for you as a friend. Nothing is more important to me than your happiness.*

He flung his phone aside after reading Shruti's message. The lengths to which she was willing to go to win him over exasperated him. But it was even more infuriating how Sevita didn't call or try to meet him at all. She was posting every day about new places she was going to with her new friends. Nitin was in every picture. He couldn't ignore it, but nor did he want to seem petty.

Finally, it was the day of Nitin's birthday party. Kunal texted Sevita saying he would pick her up at 8 p.m. She replied, hours later, that she had gone bowling.

*Can't wait! His party will be fun!*

'His party ...' Kunal murmured in disbelief.

—

Sama was in high spirits that evening as she sat surfing channels and sipping her coffee. This was the first time she had gone bowling. It was all very new and exciting. Besides that, she had been waiting for this day.

'Someone is in a good mood,' her mother said. She came with a slice of banana pie and sat down beside her. Sama shifted a little, uncomfortable.

'Yes, it is Nitin's birthday today, so we took a quick trip to his favourite bowling alley.'

'That sounds fun. Eat some more, Sevita. You hardly had any.' Mrs Vyas put her hand on Sama's shoulder, smiling as she looked at her. Sama's heart beat faster.

'I can't. I have to go to the party at his farmhouse tonight. It will be a feast.' She forced a smile. 'We plan to party all night. I better not stuff myself.'

Her mother's smile disappeared, and a worried frown appeared instead. 'I thought the party was just around here.

Baby, it doesn't look good, partying with guys all night, and that too in a far away farmhouse. Come back by midnight, won't you?'

Suddenly, Sama's blood rushed to her head. 'What do you mean? My whole class is going to be there. Lots of girls are going. Shruti will be there. Kunal's going with me.'

'I know, it's just that—'

'Just what?' Sama stood up angrily, shrugging Mrs Vyas's hand off her shoulder. 'Don't you see how suffocating this house is? Wherever I look, I see her ghost! I look at myself in the mirror, and I see her dead face! Is it so difficult to let me change the atmosphere? Do you have any clue how hard it is for me?'

Mrs Vyas was stunned into silence. Her eyes were wide with shock and guilt. Had she been mistaken in thinking that Sevita seemed to be recovering from her sister's death?

'I didn't mean to upset you. I am so sorry,' she said, watching her daughter's eyes fill with tears.

'Kunal will pick me up at eight. I'm going to get dressed.'

'But you'll keep calling me, right? I am just worried for your safety, sweetheart,' she said.

I'll text you,' Sama said defiantly as she marched out of the living room.

Mrs Vyas remained dumbstruck on the sofa. Maybe she had been insensitive towards her daughter in some way. Or was this just a teenage rebellion? She had assumed that stage had passed with Sevita, but trauma could manifest in so many ways. Mrs Vyas took a deep breath and switched channels, trying to calm her agitated nerves.

A car horn honked outside their gate a little after eight. Sama walked out of her room. Her heels clacked as she made her way through the living room. Looking up at her, Mrs Vyas saw that she was wrapped up in a long, black overcoat. She wondered what her daughter was wearing under it. Sevita would usually show her dress off and frolic around as her mother took pictures when she dressed up for an event. Maybe her mood was still off, she thought.

Mrs Vyas smiled at her.

'That's a nice bag,' she said, looking at the beaded black bag that Sama was holding.

'Thanks. I'll see you tomorrow.' Sama left without a wave or a smile.

*I hope she's not wearing anything too revealing*, she thought. She was anxious but told herself she needed to trust her daughter more. After all, she was an adult.

---

Sama walked towards Kunal's car. She could see his face glisten in the intense moonlight as he waited for her. He was in a crisp white shirt and a casual black blazer. Just looking at him made her tingle all over, but she would have to contain herself.

When she approached the car, she saw a guy from Kunal's football team in the front seat. She stopped outside the car's front door on the passenger side, a slight frown on her face.

'Whoa, why are you hiding in that coat?' Kunal's friend said with a grin. Sama bent down to the window and looked into his eyes.

'Mind moving back?'

'Sure,' he said, the grin on his face fading. He moved back, and Sama got in without glancing at Kunal. She kept her coat on as she settled in for the long ride.

'You look different,' Kunal said. He couldn't take his eyes off her flawless face. She looked stunning.

'Thanks,' she said, checking her lipstick in a small mirror she took out of her bag. Kunal had been amused when she wanted to sit in front with him, but now he felt hurt. Why wouldn't she look at him?

The farmhouse was a good thirty minutes away and deep in the woods. Throughout the drive, Sama listened to music and watched the moonlit landscape. Kunal glanced at her every now and then but couldn't catch her eye. Thankfully, his friend in the back seat kept up a pleasant conversation that kept things from getting awkward.

Eventually, they reached an ornate iron gate that was opened by a security guard to let them in. A concrete path stretched out ahead of them under a series of intricate metal arches. As they drove in, they noticed beautiful flowering creepers twisted around the arches. After a short while, they reached the porch. A valet opened the door for Sama and took the keys from Kunal with a well-practised bow.

'This is so grand!' Sama said, looking at the huge oak doors that opened into a big hall. Inside, it was all white marble lit by massive chandeliers and dotted with exotic indoor plants, like a seven-star hotel. Family portraits hung on the walls. Chatter and music filled the air that smelled of roses. Outside, near the pool area, Sama could see disco lights blinking in bright shades. A DJ played popular tracks.

'Welcome, my favourite people!' Nitin came rushing to receive them. He looked good in his rugged denim jeans, a white T-shirt and a fitted white blazer.

'Happy birthday!' Kunal smiled and gave him a hug.

'Happy birthday, Nitin! You look decent for a birthday boy,' Sama said with a brilliant smile, one that she had secretly been working on for a while.

'Thanks a lot. But it's my eighteenth, so the boy is no longer a boy!' They all laughed. 'Oh, where are my manners? May I please take your coat?' he asked Sama politely.

'Please,' Sama turned, shrugging the coat off her shoulder.

People around her went silent as if under a spell.

The coat slid down her bare shoulders. A dark blue strap glittered with sequins against her milky skin. The coat slipped further down, slowly, revealing her back. She was wearing an almost backless gown, its silky fabric fitting her like a second skin. It gently clung to her hips and fell smoothly over her legs. There was a long slit all the way up to her thigh. The black stilettos she wore were studded with glass crystals. When she turned, everything seemed to slow down. The sweetheart cut of the neckline was deep. Her collar bones shimmered as the light from the chandelier fell on her. The skin over her cleavage was paler than the rest of her body. Her hair fell in soft, silky curls down to her waist.

In that moment, she defined perfection.

Kunal caught his breath when she finally turned to look at him. He realized that everyone in the hall was looking at her.

Shruti, who had walked in minutes ago with her date, Jai, took in the spectacle. She gulped, straightening her red skater dress as she stood beside him in the middle of the hall. She noticed Jai staring at Sevita. Shruti stood as straight as she could, pulling her shoulders back and holding her head high. Why was she left embarrassed every time she thought she had let go of the past and moved on? Wasn't she enough? She felt crushed.

'Thank you, Nitin,' Sama said, moving her gaze away from Kunal, and smiling at Nitin.

'The pleasure is all mine,' Nitin answered, almost in a daze.

'I guess we should get some drinks,' Kunal said, quickly putting his arm around her and moving her away.

'You look gorgeous,' he whispered to her while trying to stare down every guy who was looking at her. 'Actually, too gorgeous for this party.'

'Oh, I didn't realize that.' She picked up a tall glass of champagne, not looking at him once again. A new friend she had made came up to talk to her. She introduced Kunal to him but was soon deep in conversation with the guy, ignoring Kunal. One after another, her new friends walked over and surrounded her, talking and laughing.

The party picked up speed as starters and drinks began circulating. People who had come in groups were soon scattered as girls and boys mingled and paired off. Those who had come with their dates were already finding corners to get cosy in. Nitin and his core group of friends were at the centre of all the party games, dancing and playing pranks. Sama was with them and cheered every time Nitin pulled a stunt.

Kunal stood silently with a forced smile on his face, watching her laugh with the other guys. Nitin juggled some shot glasses as a part of a party game while people made videos and cheered him on. Shruti cheered the loudest. Jai seemed a little put off by her behaviour, but he clapped along. Sama could see Shruti try her best to gain attention. She was talking to a lot of guys, laughing loudly and touching Jai's arm with every step she took. It was all too pitifully obvious and Sama wasn't the only one to notice that. Jai looked fed up too.

—

At around ten, a triple-decker birthday cake arrived by the poolside on a trolley. The DJ played a special birthday remix for Nitin, who couldn't be happier. He cut the cake amidst loud cheers and gestured to the bartender to bring him two bottles of champagne.

'Sevita, help me pop one? For Lady Luck?' He extended his hand towards her. He purposely ignored Kunal, who was standing right there, and grinned boyishly at Sama. Their friends and classmates were surprised; since when had the two been such close buddies?

'Why not?' She took his hand and gave him a brilliant smile. Nitin handed her a bottle of Rosé champagne. Together, they popped the two bottles and sprinkled it on everyone as far as the fizz would go.

'Cheers to life, guys!'

'Cheers!' people shouted, raising their glasses high. Kunal stood in a dark spot at a distance. He needed something stronger than champagne. What was going on? Was he overreacting?

Meanwhile, as she watched Sama become the life of the party and take countless pictures with Nitin, Shruti felt dejected. *Sevita already has Kunal, and yet a popular guy like Nitin is also interested in her*, she thought. *What is so special about her?* Jai had left her side to join his friends for drinks. Shruti wished Astha was there. If only Astha's parents weren't so orthodox. Amidst the noise and the crowd, she felt completely alone and defeated.

After the revelry, Sama took her tall glass of champagne and walked towards a seat at the poolside bar. She was conscious of people's eyes on her.

'Enjoying the party?' Nitin sat beside her, holding his third drink.

'Yeah, thanks to you!'

'I hope you enjoyed the Rosé. Dad got it from France recently. It's vintage. Very special ... like you are. I'm glad you came today.' Clearly, Nitin was drunk.

'I'm glad I came too, Nitin. Cheers!' Sama said charmingly, raising her glass. She could see Kunal across the pool. He had been standing there for several minutes, observing her. She wanted him to watch her a little more, and suffer like she had.

'I've been thinking, what if I had met you earlier?' said Nitin, 'Everything could have been so different ...'

'Is that so? I wonder how,' she replied with a shrug. She could see Kunal from the corner of her eye. Finally, Kunal could stand it no longer. He put his glass on a table and walked away.

---

How did it come to this? Kunal was hurting with a pain he'd never felt before. It was not just jealousy or insecurity; it was something more. With his hands in his pockets, he walked away from the crowd, staring blankly at the sky. The night was dark blue, like her gown, he thought. The stars were like the sequins on her dress. It was a beautiful night with a full moon and few clouds. The weather was clear, and the air was cold.

Moonlight seeped through a thick cluster of trees behind the farmhouse. He walked towards it. It was darker here. Kunal stopped beneath a tall tree standing like a shadow against the sky, and took a deep breath. The noise, the party chatter and Nitin's face slowly faded. He let the serenity fill him, but his heart was breaking. The brave front he was keeping up crumbled as he closed his eyes tightly. Was he losing her?

'Hi ...'

Kunal snapped out of his reverie and turned. There she was, slowly making her way towards him, her stilettos hanging from her hands as she walked barefoot. Her body swayed like the willowy trees of the woods. Her eyes gleamed in the moonlight. The soft breeze pushed her hair back, baring her shoulders. The thin strap of her dress glittered dark blue. She seemed surreal, like the magic that comes alive in a forest at night.

'Hi,' he managed to say, his voice serious. 'I thought you were busy.'

'Well, I had company, but not the kind I wanted.' She stopped an arm's length away from him. 'I didn't see you around, so I looked, and here you are in the most alluring spot on this property,' she said, looking around. His eyes were fixed on her. She couldn't say if they were cold or burning.

'Do you love me?' he asked abruptly.

'Do you?' she asked, returning his gaze. He stepped closer to her. For a split second, Sama was scared. Something was different about him.

'Do I love you?' He tightly grabbed her arm. Her stilettos fell from her hand. She gasped. Her eyes were wide in surprise. He grasped her shoulder with one hand and pulled her hair with the other as he kissed her passionately. The force of his body pushed her against the tree.

'I hate to see you with any other guy,' he said and kissed her neck, sucking her skin. 'I hate it when they look at you,' he said, biting her shoulder. She gasped again, clutching his shirt. His body was pressed against her. She could hardly breathe or move. He pushed her strap out of the way and pulled her neckline further down roughly. She gasped again, but the pain felt good. It was the first time he had taken control. She could feel his skin become feverishly hot. Her heart raced, and her head was fuzzy.

'I hate it when you question my love for you,' he pressed

hard on her lips again, sliding his hand under the slit of her gown, grabbing her thigh. 'You still want to know if I love you?' She gasped again as his hands ran up her thigh, making her moan.

'Yes,' she said. 'I want to know.' Sama sighed as he pressed her harder against the tree. She put her arms around him. In the heat of the moment, they didn't care where they were, or who could see them. Sama unzipped him, and he grabbed her waist, sweat dripping from his forehead in the cold breeze. She gasped with every thrust that pushed her against the bark of the tree, and she moaned as he went deeper.

---

Some distance away, in the faintly lit backyard of the farmhouse, Shruti stood rooted to the spot. She was facing the woods, looking at Kunal and Sama. At that moment, she caught Sama's eye. Sama was looking at her with a smirk on her face.

'How much do you love me?' she whispered in Kunal's ear, making him push harder.

'More than you know,' he gasped in the throes of passion.

Shruti's blood ran cold. She had followed Kunal when he had left the party all alone. He looked upset, and Shruti had noticed Sevita sitting with Nitin. It was an opportunity to talk to him, but before she could approach Kunal, Sevita had reached him. What had ensued broke her completely.

*I'm sure she saw me. She was looking down on me,* the thoughts buzzed in her head. Shruti turned away and walked back to the party. A feeling of emptiness coursed through her veins. She felt breathless. Her hands trembled. She pushed a few guys away from the bar and got herself a glass of whiskey. And then another. After a while, her head started spinning.

Shruti somehow made it to the ladies' room. The moment she closed the door of the first vacant stall behind her, she puked. Her head hurt, and her body felt heavy and cold. Her stomach hurt too. The acrid taste in her throat sickened her. She somehow cleaned up and walked out. In a corner of the washroom, she sat on a stool with her head in her hands. All she could hear was her own rapid breathing. Shruti was glad no one came in. If they saw her in such a sorry state, it would be embarrassing.

'Oh! This is where you've been hiding.'

Shruti looked up and saw Sevita. Her eyes fell on the hickeys all over her neck and chest. She had made no effort to hide them. Her hair was tousled, sticking to her sweaty skin. Her gown was dishevelled, and her face was flushed. There was a big smile on her face. Shruti had never seen her friend smile like that before.

'Thank god for waterproof makeup. The heat of his body melts me,' Sevita said as she brushed her hair.

Shruti shivered. Did she hear that right?

'What?'

'I said the heat of this party melts me. My makeup would be all runny if it wasn't waterproof.'

'Oh, right.'

'Like yours, you know. The liner and kajal are ...' She indicated the mess on Shruti's face with her fingers, frowning in disgust. 'Shruti, some people can never get what they want. But don't take it too badly. Why don't you try focusing on some of your strong points like ... well ....' Her eyes squinted as she searched for words. '...I am sure there's something.'

She shrugged indifferently as she picked up her clutch and started to walk out

'Oh, I almost forgot.' She turned to Shruti one last time. 'Your dress? It makes you look fatter than you are. You need to choose according to your size.' There was contempt in her tone. With a final smirk, she left.

Shruti was too shocked to react. She hadn't expected this from Sevita. After what seemed like hours, she got up and looked into the mirror. Sevita was right. The face that looked back at her was a mess. A fat face streaked with runny makeup. She splashed some water and washed it all off. Then she applied her makeup again and looked at herself in the mirror. No amount of effort made any difference to her round, unhappy face.

—

It was almost midnight, and the party was raging. Sevita and Kunal were holding each other close and dancing. Shruti watched the two as they danced, lost to the world. The reality had hit her that night. The scene of the two lovers had jolted her. Holding back her tears, she looked around for Jai. He was getting a hookah ready. She patted her face, straightened her dress and walked up to him.

'Which flavour?' she asked him, flashing a needy smile. He had asked her out. Surely, he wanted to be with her.

'Apple and mint. You want to join us?' he asked a little hesitantly, glancing at his friends in a corner. Shruti laughed drunkenly.

'I want to join you,' she said, trying to sound seductive. She stepped closer to him, swaying. 'Let's go somewhere more private—'

Jai stepped back from her and said, 'You've got it all wrong, Shruti. I'm not interested in you like that.' He looked horrified.

'What do you mean? You asked me out!' Her heart beat faster.

'Yes, but this is not what I wanted. It's our first date, for heaven's sake.' He frowned at her.

'You said you liked me.' Her face heated up.

'Yeah, and I can see that was a mistake. Do you have no shame?'

His frown turned to a scowl, and he stormed away. The group of boys in the corner sniggered. Shruti had noticed their presence too late.

Shruti walked to the other end of the pool, shivering. Someone's half-drunk cocktail was left on a table. She gulped it in one go. The whirling humiliation inside her wouldn't die down. Jai's scowling face swam in front of her eyes. His words resounded in her mind.

*Do you have no shame?*

A classmate found her in her pitiful condition and offered to drop her home. She stood up without a word and followed the guy out.

She was silent throughout the drive back home. Her stomach turned every time she replayed the image of Jai glaring at her. She felt like a failure every time she remembered Sevita's perfect face sneering at her. Kunal's heavy breathing and her ecstatic moans echoed in her ears. Shruti's heart was broken.

She could still recall the first time she had met Kunal in high school. He had introduced himself with a smile that had melted her heart. It still did. His pearly white teeth and his deep brown eyes made her fall head over heels in love with him. But he would never be hers. Shruti knew now that she would never be good enough—not for Kunal nor for anyone else.

She felt alone. Maybe, she'd feel better once she was home, she thought.

She was wrong.

---

It was almost 2 a.m. when she rang the doorbell. Her father came to the door, grumbling. He was not pleased to see her. He hadn't wanted her to go in the first place, and now he'd had to get out of bed in the middle of the night to open the door for her. Not only that, she smelled of puke and whiskey. Her father was in shock. He had forbidden her to drink.

He glowered at her. She was a disgrace. She looked like a whore in that short dress, he shouted. Why did she have to expose her legs when she was so fat? He screamed at the top of his lungs. He kept screaming angrily as she walked past him, stiff as a board, and started up the stairs. Her mother also came out of the bedroom. Shruti saw on her face the same expression of disgust that Sevita wore whenever she had looked at her, back at the party.

'These horrible habits you've formed in college are why you won't get a good marksheet! You will be the biggest failure in this family!' The shouting continued.

She closed the door of her room. She could still hear him shouting. Her mother was trying to pacify him and asking him to go back to sleep. Her room was dark and unbearably quiet. She could feel her ears pulsate. She took off her shoes and walked out onto her balcony. The cold breeze fluttered in her hair and sang softly as if trying to heal her scorching skin. Her eyes were still burning, but the tears wouldn't roll down. Somewhere far away, a dog was howling. Crickets were shrieking from the corners they hid in.

Shruti stepped over the balcony grill and jumped.

# BUTTERFLIES IN A JAR

It was past three in the morning when the party was finally over. Sama had changed into a comfortable pullover and pyjamas. She cuddled with Kunal on a single bed as he ran his fingers through her hair.

The people staying over had shared beds in a big room. Many were still talking about the party, announcing awards for the most drunk, the most wasted and so on. Someone laughed, recalling how Shruti had made a fool of herself.

'She was drunk, that's all. Stop it,' Jai snapped.

Kunal was surprised to know about Shruti's drunken state. As far as he knew, she wasn't allowed to drink and respected her family's rules.

'Who dropped her back?' Kunal asked.

'Dunno, some guy from the front benches,' Jai said, still annoyed.

'Kunal, I'm sure she's okay,' Sama said, holding his face in her hands.

'Yeah.' He kissed her head and put his arms around her. He felt at peace with the world; the woman he loved was in his arms, and there was nothing else between them. Sama let him caress her hair. Killing two birds with one stone felt good. Not only had she managed to get Kunal back that night, but she had also been able to keep Shruti at bay.

She had seen Shruti follow Kunal as he left the pool area. That sneaky bitch was trying to catch Kunal alone. She had immediately taken off her heels so she could walk fast, and slipped away, unnoticed, from the party.

Sama spotted Shruti standing in a corner, behind the house, watching Kunal from a distance. She was obviously thinking of what to say when she approached him. Before Shruti could make a move, Sama hurried towards Kunal. She knew Shruti was watching them. She was thrilled at Kunal's sudden rush of passion, but what satisfied her more was the disturbed expression on Shruti's face as she saw them.

She wouldn't dare interfere between them ever again.

---

The next day was a Saturday, and no one wanted to go to college after the previous night's partying. But there was an important Math class in the morning, so, except for those with serious hangovers, everyone made it on time.

'What is happening?' Kunal stopped in his tracks in the corridor leading to the classroom. A policeman was standing right outside their door. Sama clutched his arm.

'I don't like this,' she said with a practised worried expression.

Sama's eyes fell on Inspector Mohite standing in the middle of the class. A sense of alarm overtook her. What was he doing there?

Their professor was standing beside the inspector, looking visibly shaken. When almost everyone had arrived and taken their seats, Mohite cleared his throat loudly.

'I have some bad news,' his baritone echoed through the classroom. 'One of your friends, Shruti Jain, died around 2 a.m. today.'

Kunal froze in his chair. Jai's eyes widened as if he had been struck by lightning. Nitin and his group of friends looked shocked, while Astha burst into loud sobs.

Sama was shocked too.

She had thought Shruti would simply stay out of her way, but now she had gone and died? This was not according to plan. She was irked.

'This unfortunate event happened after a birthday party last night. We'll have to question everyone in the class, especially those who were at this party. I hope you will all cooperate with us and come to the principal's room when called. We'll start with Nitin.'

Nitin blanched at his name being announced but got up and went with the inspector.

Messages started floating on the WhatsApp group made for Nitin's birthday party. Links to news articles were being circulated. Shruti's father had found her lying dead on the lawn. He was so shocked that he had fainted on the spot and had to be hospitalized.

One by one, the students were called in. Nitin did not return to the classroom after his interrogation. Jai returned looking terrified. When Astha came back, her eyes were swollen and red. She looked scathingly at Sama before grabbing her bag and walking out of the classroom. Sama was sure something was not right. She waited for Kunal. At last, he came back after a long session in the principal's room.

'What did he ask?'

'A lot of questions—my relationship with her, how long I'd known her, what happened at the party ... I don't get it, Sevita. Why did she do it?' He sat on the desk, fidgeting nervously. 'Maybe it was also because ... I was rude to her some days back.'

'Don't blame yourself, Kunal. She was not very sensitive towards your feelings either. Plus, that was weeks ago. We didn't even speak to her after that.'

'Exactly, we weren't there for her.' He shook his head in dismay.

Sama was annoyed. All her hard work had been for nothing. She sighed impatiently, waiting her turn. She knew she could handle it this time. After all, she had not done anything.

Not directly.

---

'We meet again,' Inspector Mohite said, his hawkish stare regarding Sama's poker face. The principal's room had been cleared for the interviews. There were only a few chairs and a table with a notepad, a pen and a recorder on it. Vikrant Singh was assisting Mohite.

'Unfortunately, in these circumstances,' Sama said with measured sadness as she took a seat.

'How would you describe your relationship with Shruti?'

'We were good friends, always together in school and college. She was like a sister to me ... until Sama's death. After that, things have been different for everyone—'

'Different how?'

'Maybe it was my fault,' she sighed sorrowfully. 'After Sama's death, I became too needy. I wanted my friends to be with me all the time. You see, I've never felt so lonely. Even if Sama never talked much, she was always there. Anyway, after a few days of being by my side, Shruti got annoyed. She said she had other priorities and couldn't always be with me. I was hurt ... so we were not really talking.'

'When did she say this?'

'Around three weeks back, in Pune. We'd gone to a college fest together. I could never imagine she would do this ... just like I couldn't with my sister ...'

She bit her lip and looked down at the floor, her eyes moist. Vijay shifted in his chair, but Mohite pressed on regardless.

'I see. So you wouldn't know if she'd been having any problems lately, or about any recent changes in her behaviour?'

'No, nothing I can point to. Except the party.'

'What happened at the party?'

'Well, we were all having a great time, celebrating Nitin's birthday. Shruti ... I don't know how to say this.' She frowned slightly before continuing. 'People were saying she was quite drunk. That she had asked Jai to get intimate with her, and he had refused. In fact, I even saw her puke in the washroom before that. Maybe Jai's rejection pushed her—'

'You're telling me you saw her in that state and yet did nothing to help her?' Mohite asked pointedly. Anger shot through her like a wave.

*I won't fall into your trap and get agitated, Inspector.*

'No, she said she didn't need my help. Didn't want anything to do with me,' Sama responded with a pained look.

'So you didn't bother to check on her later?'

'I felt quite hurt by her response, so no. Afterwards, I got busy with my friends. She had her own date, or so I thought. She was all over him last night. Anyone could see that.'

'How long had Jai been dating her?'

'I guess just a week? I think he asked her out to have a date for the party. Maybe Astha would know; she was closer to her.'

'According to Astha, Shruti was having trouble with you. Was there a cold war going on?'

'Cold war?' she chuckled. 'I don't have that kind of time.'

'What happened in the Chemistry class?'

*So that's what Astha told him.*

'Shruti and I were grouped together for a pop quiz. She didn't know the answers and was stressed about losing marks. So I answered the ones I knew. She even thanked me for it later.'

'Let's go back to what happened last night. You didn't notice that she had disappeared from the party?'

'It did cross my mind, but I thought she would be with Jai. Couples had occupied the peaceful corners of the farmhouse.'

'Where were you?'

'With my friends.'

'Where exactly in the farmhouse?'

'Around the pool, in the hall, went to the bathroom a couple of times. Then in the master bedroom on the first floor, where we all shared beds and extra mattresses for a sleepover.'

'Who all were you with?'

'Mostly Nitin and his group of friends. Why?' She shifted in her seat.

'Who dropped her back?' Mohite asked, ignoring her.

'I'm not sure. I didn't see.'

'Did anything else happen?' he asked, spinning a pen between his thumb and index finger. Sama pressed her lips together as if she was thinking hard.

'There was this thing. I heard that when Jai turned her down, a group of guys saw the whole thing and laughed at her. Well, everyone was drunk and being silly. I hope you won't hold these little mistakes against anyone.'

'Why not? I don't think it is right to embarrass a person for any reason.'

For a fraction of a second, Sama watched him. She sensed that his piercing eyes and the impatient fingers rotating the pen were calculated gestures, all designed to intimidate. Well, it wouldn't work on her anymore.

'Sir, I didn't want to say this, but she was not a happy girl. Her parents put a lot of pressure on her to excel in studies, in sports ... everything. They weren't even happy with how she looked and had made her join a gym.' Her brows came together in a pained, anxious frown.

Sama had heard Shruti tell Sevita all this while eavesdropping on them about a year ago. Sevita had always been kind to Shruti because of her family issues.

'I see. A neighbour did say they heard some shouting last night,' the inspector said casually, his sharp eyes still on her. 'Is there anything else you want to tell me?'

'Just that the group who laughed at her may have been silly, but they didn't mean any harm. In fact, Jai put a stop to their sniggering immediately. These things are not meant to be taken seriously. I know sometimes it can get too much for a person, like it happened with my sister. But Shruti? I could never imagine she would do such a thing.' She let out another heavy sigh, rubbing her forehead. Maintaining the expression of grief on her face was beginning to exhaust her. 'Is there anything else you want to ask?'

'Not right now. You may go. Thanks for cooperating with us.'

She stood up, shook his hand with a slight nod and left the room. Mohite stood silently contemplative as he watched her go.

---

Shruti's funeral was a sad affair. Her mother was wailing inside the house. Many of Shruti's friends and classmates, including people who were at the party the previous night, were there, their faces ash-grey. Astha was there too. She gave Sama searing glances through her tears. Shruti's father was still in the hospital. The air was heavy with grief. For Sama, it was simply a waste of time.

'I can't breathe, Kunal.' Sama feigned dizziness to escape the oppressive atmosphere. She was not in the least interested in watching Shruti's mother beat her chest and cry.

'Let's leave,' Kunal said. He was disturbed at the state Shruti's mother was in. 'I need a smoke today.'

Wordlessly they drove out towards the hills, a packet of cigarettes balancing on the dashboard. Sama joined him for a smoke, sitting on the car's hood. She was pissed off that Shruti, even in death, was trying to take Kunal away from her. After a few hours, he dropped her home with a hug and a kiss. That day, Sama didn't mind being alone in her room. There was something she had to do.

---

Astha left Shruti's house a little after Kunal and Sama. She had to see Andrew and let it all out.

She covered her head with the hood of her jacket as she walked into the woods on the hill near Sama's house. She looked around, making sure no one had followed her.

'Andrew!' she sighed in relief when she saw a tall, thin figure standing near the rusted gate of the house. She ran into his arms. He held her tight and kissed her.

'Goodness! Are you all right?' he said as he hugged her. She swayed for a moment and broke down in tears. He led her to the porch across the lawn. He had cleaned the cracked marble floor and placed a portable mattress there. She sat down with him and cried into his chest.

'It's terrible what happened, but you need to calm down. I can't watch you cry like this.' he said and caressed her face. She was feverish from all the sobbing.

'Andrew, there is something I want to show you. She messaged me on Facebook before she did it.' Andrew blinked in surprise. 'What do you mean?' he asked.

'I ... I took screenshots and deleted all the messages from her account and mine.'

'What?'

'I knew her password.'

'But why did you delete them?'

'Because if they dig deeper, they will see that I was the last person she messaged. They would question me, maybe even find out about us. I can't have that, not till you are ready.'

'Astha ...' Andrew shook his head. He was terrified by what she had done. She had tampered with evidence. If the police found out, she would be in bigger trouble than she thought. 'What did she say, though?'

'Look, it was Sevita.' She gave him her phone. He looked at the screenshots, his eyes squinting in disbelief as he read.

---

*Once again, Astha, you were not there when I needed you the most. I am embarrassed, ashamed of what I am and what I did. I looked fat, I acted like a whore, and I was stupid enough to think he would consider my feelings. I saw him with her. I saw them making out in the woods. I saw her look at me. I saw the contempt in her eyes. I can't help but feel like a loser. She's right, no one wants me. My mom and dad hate me. Even you said I overthink everything. Yesterday, you told me to forget the past and enjoy the party. I tried to do just that. I let Jai take me along as a date only to be laughed at. He said I had no shame.*

*I don't know what to do or how to live anymore. Maybe if you were there, if you saw what happened, you would understand. She's made me realize how inferior I am. How can I carry on like this? I have to get out of this place.*

*You will help me, won't you?*

'Sevita let her watch them?' Astha covered her quivering lips with her hand. 'How could she? She knew how madly Shruti loved Kunal. It almost killed her when they got together. Shruti had told me that she had been putting her down for weeks. What more did she do at the party? And I wasn't there for her either.' Tears streamed down her cheeks yet again. 'She was opening her heart to me, and I told her she was overthinking.'

'Astha.' Andrew held her shoulders gently and looked into her eyes. 'You can't blame yourself. How could you have known? If you want, you can show this to the police.'

'And soil her name? What would people think of her? And if the police find out about us, if some clue leads them to you and me, we'll be over. You know my father's temper. His family name and honour are more valuable to him than my life. Who knows what he'll do?'

She sobbed again. Andrew held her, feeling powerless. Astha was right. Her father was an influential politician. If they were not careful, he'd be found dead in a pit.

'You're right. Whatever we do, it won't bring Shruti back. But keep the screenshots in case we need them later. You know, it does seem like Sevita almost pushed her into a breakdown. It wasn't just her parents.'

'Why? The Sevita I know could never do something like that.' Astha looked at him, perturbed.

'From what you've told me, it seems she hasn't been the same since her sister died. Anyway, please let all this go,' he implored her. 'You need to look after yourself.'

He kissed her as she put her arms around him. It had been days since she had seen him. They lay down on the mattress and made love under the cloudy sky.

---

From the comfort of her bed, enjoying a cup of coffee, Sama closed her tab after making a copy of the recording. She had been watching the secret date the whole time. The camera that used to be in Sevita's room was now installed in the ruins of the old house, with a clear view of the porch, where she had first seen Astha meet her secret lover. Sama had known it would come in handy one day.

*Andrew.* She began looking him up online. Astha didn't have any social media accounts, so it was a bit difficult to find him. Once she had managed to track him down, however, she discovered that he was from Pune, a student at a university not far from Lavasa. He was an average boy from an average family and had many friends who played in small-time heavy metal bands. He wasn't a challenge to deal with. As for the messages Astha had with her, such evidence could be easily refuted. It didn't bother her. But Astha herself ...

*It's time to teach her a lesson,* said the voice in her head.

---

Kunal was in no mood to go to college, but he was also concerned about Sevita. Losing her sister and then her friend could not have been easy. He had to make sure she was okay. He picked her up as always. He didn't say much on the drive. Though he was trying to act normal, sadness and guilt tore at him.

The atmosphere in college was grim. Many seats in the classroom were empty. Nitin and Jai were absent. Astha hadn't come either. The day dragged on as one monotonous lecture followed another. Sama felt her spirits sink with every glance at Kunal. He seemed distracted. The distance between them was excruciating.

When the lunch bell finally rang at one o'clock, Kunal got up quickly and slung his bag over his shoulder.

'Sevita, could you get me some sandwiches? I'll see you in the canteen.'

'Sure.'

Sama didn't know what it was, but something wasn't right.

Kunal walked rapidly towards the parking lot, confused yet curious to know what was going on.

*Can you come out alone to the parking lot? Need to talk to you about Shruti.*

---

Astha had messaged him while he was in class. Maybe she didn't want Sevita to hear anything that would make her feel worse? He reached his car and stood there, waiting. Astha appeared five minutes later. She looked scared and panicky.

'Astha, are you okay?'

'We need to talk. Where is Sevita?'

'She's not here. You asked me to come alone.'

'This is going to sound odd. But it's no coincidence that Shruti got depressed after the party.'

'I know,' he sighed.

'You know?' Astha was surprised.

'Yes, but it was too late. If I had known those guys had laughed at her, or that she was going through such a bad phase—'

'Not that, Kunal! Shruti had a fight with Sevita. Did you not notice something odd after the college fest?'

He frowned. All he could recall was how Sevita had made it the most memorable night of his life.

'No, nothing odd. Why?'

'Shruti stopped speaking to you two. Can't you recall that?' Astha nearly shouted.

'Wait a minute. Shruti didn't stop speaking to us. I distanced myself from her. Besides, we did not have time for her. Every time I spoke to her, she tried to badmouth Sevita. Of course, I didn't know about her depression. I swear I would have—'

'Kunal, think about it. Why would she badmouth Sevita?'

'Isn't that obvious?' He shrugged, irritated.

'Open your eyes, Kunal. Don't you think Sevita has changed? Can't you see that she's no longer the person that she was? Or are you that blind?'

'Well, she saw her sister die. What exactly is your point?' He was angry now.

'How can a person change fundamentally? It's odd. The way she behaves, the way she put Shruti down at the fest and humiliated her in the chemistry quiz—'

'That chemistry quiz? Are you serious?' He chuckled in disbelief. 'She answered a few basic questions, and that hurt Shruti's pride?'

'It wasn't the questions. It was the way she looked at her!' Astha shook her head, frustrated.

'Astha, I understand that everything is scary for you right now. I feel that way too. But please stop making things harder.'

Astha took a deep breath. Kunal wouldn't understand till he saw for himself.

'I think I should show you.' She took her phone out and unlocked it. Astha wasn't sure whether Shruti's last message would make any difference at all, but she had to try. Her trembling fingers swiped through the pictures in her gallery. Maybe once Kunal saw those screenshots, he would understand.

'Kunal, here you are.'

Astha gasped, almost dropping her phone. Sevita had arrived on the scene.

'Astha?' Her voice was soft and apprehensive, her eyes moist. 'I thought you didn't come today. What's going on?'

Astha stepped back, clutching her phone.

'What are you doing here?' she spat, trembling with an inexplicable fear.

'I ... couldn't find my wallet,' Sama looked at Kunal, a hurt expression on her face. 'I thought maybe it was in your car. I had no idea you and Astha ... would be here.' She was breathing unevenly as if scarred by some deep personal trauma.

'Sevita, it's okay. I think Astha is just having a hard time coming to terms with the truth,' Kunal said and glowered at Astha. 'Shruti was depressed, and her suicide is nobody's fault.'

There was a long silence.

'I can't stand this anymore,' Sama finally said in a shaky voice. 'I'm leaving. You guys can catch up all you want.' A tear rolled down her cheek. She turned and started to walk away.

'Sevita, wait!' Kunal called after her. 'You should just go home now and stop with these accusations,' he told Astha sternly before he ran behind Sama.

Astha was stunned into silence. It was as if Kunal was blindfolded. Maybe she could send him the screenshots later, and that would knock some sense into him.

—

After having lunch at a café, Kunal took Sama for a long drive. They drove around the town and then headed to the outskirts. A light rain came down, dancing with the sun and the clouds. A breeze with the fragrance of the hills blew across them as they drove. Kunal stopped in a deserted corner and leaned over to kiss her.

'Have I told you I love you?'

'Hmm, not in a few days.' Sama smiled.

'That's unforgivable. I should say it every day. Let me make it up to you.' He kissed her again, feeling her flawless body with his fingertips.

Sama had been waiting for this. Finally Kunal was out of the rut Shruti's death had thrown him into, thanks to Astha. She let him push the seats back and unbutton her shirt. She let him kiss her passionately, please her in every way and make love to her. He was the only person who made her feel alive.

'Did I say I love you too?' she whispered in his ear as he wrapped her in his arms. Hours had passed by.

He smiled and rested his head on her shoulder. 'Let's go eat something and come back here.'

'But why are we coming back? We can go to my room,' Sama offered.

'I have camping gear in the back. From Dad's weekend trip with his friends. Why don't we camp? Stargaze and hold hands?'

'You're sure you can just hold hands?' she smiled and glanced at him. He laughed. She watched his eyes twinkle. For a moment, she forgot to breathe.

—

'Mom didn't have a problem with my staying out tonight. As for Dad, he's been working a lot lately,' Sama told Kunal as they lay together on a mattress, gazing up at the ink-blue sky dotted with stars. 'I think he's still coping with Sama's death.'

'Everyone has their own way of grieving.' Kunal held her hand.

'Yeah, I guess that was Astha's way of grieving. Blaming me for not entertaining Shruti's whims. I don't think I did anything wrong,' she said.

'Let her feel what she wants to. She needs time to recover, too,' Kunal said, glancing sideways at her. He couldn't help noticing that the words she chose were different from what Sevita would normally say under these circumstances. Her tone and expressions were unusually bland too. Or were Astha's words taking effect?

'Yeah, or maybe, I will try and speak to Astha about it. Make her feel better.' She smiled and looked at him, squeezing his hand.

Kunal sighed. He was definitely overthinking things, he thought. She's still caring and thoughtful. Why would Astha even suggest such things? Didn't people react differently to difficult situations? As these thoughts buzzed in his head, she suddenly kissed his hand.

'Thanks for being there for me,' she said.

Those deep, bright eyes made his heart flutter. Her gaze was enough to make him feel warm and loved. There was a new mysterious air to her. Their relationship had started to feel mature. He couldn't stay away.

'I do want to do more than just hold hands with you.' He said with a gentle kiss.

It was eleven at night. Kunal was curled around Sama, fast asleep. Sama was watching the stars, caressing his arm, when his phone vibrated. She reached out for it, careful not to wake Kunal, and unlocked it with his thumb. It was Astha. She had sent him screenshots of Shruti's message. Though her temper shot up for a second, Sama smirked after reading the message. She simply deleted it and blocked Astha on Kunal's phone.

She had gone too far. She would have to be taught a lesson.

# DARKEST AFTER DAWN

Breathing heavily, Astha pulled Andrew closer. As he kissed her neck and moved lower, the incident from the previous day flashed through her mind. The worry on Sevita's face, those eyes shining with tears, they were too perfect. Andrew moaned as he pushed against her body. After a while he rolled off, panting.

'What happened?' she asked him.

'You are not yourself today. Are you thinking about what happened in college?' he asked. Astha stared at the sky. That sense of foreboding just wouldn't go away. She nodded silently.

'You did what you could, Astha. Now let it go! Shruti won't come back whatever you do.' He caressed her face.

'Kunal didn't even reply to those screenshots. How could he be so blind?' She shut her eyes, sighing. 'I'm sorry I'm so out of it.'

'Hey, that doesn't matter right now. All I need is for you to be okay.' Andrew put his arm under her head, pulling the covers over her bare shoulders. She buried her face in his chest. If only she could be with him and forget about everything else. Her life was becoming unbearable. Suddenly, her phone rang. The blood drained from her face when she saw it was her mother calling.

'It's only twelve ... Mom knows I should be in class ... She never calls me at this time,' Astha stuttered. She shook in fear. Andrew sat up beside her.

'Just pick up and say you are on your way home early as you are not feeling well,' Andrew advised calmly, though his heart was racing. Astha picked up when it rang the second time, her voice trembling.

'Hello?'

---

'Where are you? Tell me right now.'

Her face turned ash-white. It was her father on the phone. Her throat felt constricted.

'SPEAK!' he shouted. She twitched in fear.

'I'm on my way home, Dad. I'm not feeling well,' she squeaked, her lungs collapsing in panic. Why was he calling her?

'Where exactly are you?'

'On the road. When you take the first left from the bridge,' she lied, her voice barely audible.

'I'm coming there. Stay at the bus stop.'

He hung up. Astha and Andrew stared at each other, completely horrified. What could have happened? Astha got dressed in seconds, tied her hair in a ponytail, and picked up her stuff. Andrew squeezed her hand tightly before she left.

'I hope I see you soon ...' Astha's lips trembled. She pulled her hand out of his grasp and left.

---

Astha reached the bus stop and parked her scooty. Seconds later, her dad's SUV appeared. A prominent political party's stickers were pasted on the car's front and back windshields. She knew it was serious when she saw that her father was in the driver's seat, his expression stormy. Her mother was sitting next to him with a frightened look on her face.

'Get in the car,' he rumbled in his deep voice.

She followed the order immediately. No one spoke a word till they reached the house. To her surprise, not a single servant was present. The gardener, the two maids and the errand boy were all missing. The moment her mother closed the door, her father turned towards her and slapped her hard. She shrieked as she fell to the floor.

'Stop! Please let her say something first,' her mother begged him, falling on her knees beside her daughter.

'This dirty bitch wants to ruin the family's name!' he raged. Astha trembled, tears streaming down her burning left cheek.

'Where were you for the last two days? You were not in college!'

Astha's eyes widened in horror. How did he know?

'Surprised?' He sat on a chair nearby, looking down at her with his mad red eyes.

'I got a phone call from your friend who was concerned about your absence after Shruti's death. I was shocked to learn that you had lied to us. And even more shocked—no, ashamed—to find out that you had been lying before her death too! Now tell me, where have you been going behind my back?'

Astha was petrified. Was this really happening? She was so terrorized, she couldn't move.

'What are you staring at my face for? We went to your college. We had a word with your teachers, so don't even bother denying anything. Where the hell were you all these days?' He emphasized every single word, glaring at her.

'I-I ... used to go with Shruti ... sometimes ... we bunked classes and sat in the library.'

'How convenient. You used to go with Shruti, and the dead cannot speak. Maybe I should go and put in a request for CCTV footage of college entries and exits, library and corridors. Match her rolls with your days of absence. What do you say?' His fist curled.

'I-I did not do anything you wouldn't like. I just ... wanted to hang out with friends ... that's all ...' Her voice shook. Her father's face flushed red.

'Hang out with friends? Who are these friends? Tell me the name of someone who is alive.'

'Dad, I'm sorry. Please don't be so angry,' she sobbed. 'I won't go anywhere anymore!'

'Shut up!' His voice reverberated in the empty house. 'Of course you are not going anywhere anymore!' He grabbed her arm. She screamed in pain as he dragged her to her room and flung her on the floor. 'If you don't want to study, you can just stay at home. Your mother wanted you to graduate. I wasn't for it! Now, I'll do what should be done with a daughter your age.'

Astha lay on the floor and sobbed, holding her throbbing arm as he locked the door from the outside. She had left her phone in her bag in the hall. Thankfully, there was a password, and she had deleted all evidence of Andrew from it. The screenshots were hidden away in her cloud files. She got up and wiped her tears, turning her iPad on.

'No!' she sobbed again. Her father had switched

the internet off. How would she tell Andrew what had happened? The iPad SIM only received incoming calls. She had never been allowed to have digital accounts beyond her allowance in cash. There was no way for her to recharge the number for calling. She collapsed on her bed and cried for hours. She was trapped.

In the evening, her mother unlocked the door and brought her some milk and sweet bread.

'Astha, why did you do this? You knew what would happen. Now I can't do anything to change his mind.'

'Change his mind about what?' she asked in a voice that was raspy from crying for hours.

'He's going to marry you off,' she sighed. 'I wanted you to study, have more time to yourself, but there is little I can do now. '

'Don't say that, Maa!' she clutched her mother's hand. 'Please! I can't marry, not now. I'm not ready for it.'

'You are eighteen. Women in our family get married at this age. I tried to protect you, but I can't anymore.' She gently disengaged her arm. It pained her to see her daughter in this state. 'He's waiting for his tea. I should go,' she said sadly.

'Maa ... Maa! Please don't do this to me.'

'You shouldn't have gone against his rules, Astha. I'm helpless now,' her mother said, almost weeping, and locked the door. Astha was frozen. Her head was numb.

'That bitch ... it is that bitch who called Dad,' she whispered to herself. 'Why would she call him? Why not Mom? Because she knew this would happen.'

Astha tried to calm down and gather her wits. She knew she had to find a way to tell the police about the screenshots now, whatever it took. If only she could go online, she could contact the police. She took the iPad in her hands and stared at the Wi-Fi bar, hoping and praying.

---

On the other side of the hill, Sama was with Kunal in her room. They were sitting on her bed and looking at all the pictures they had taken on their dates and during their camping trip.

'Oh wow! There's a sexy woman right there!'

Kunal had clicked a picture of her wrapped in just a towel.

'Yeah? I've got hotter ones for you if you want to see ...'

He chuckled and tickled her. She tried to control her laughter.

'Someone will wake up! Stop it.' She hit his hand. He smiled and cuddled her.

'Tell me, do you feel bad even now when I leave for home?' Kunal asked.

'Of course.' She looked into his eyes and pouted. 'If only we could live together,' she said, touching his lips.

'I want the same thing. Every day, all my life, as I said when I gave you the necklace.'

She blinked. What necklace was he talking about?

'Yeah.' She smiled quickly.

'Speaking of which, let's do a Titanic photoshoot.' He slid over her, kissing her shoulder, 'One picture, just you and the necklace, what say?'

She tried to buy some time. 'Aren't you in a naughty mood ...'

'You like the idea, don't you?' He kissed her deeply. 'Take it out. I want to see you in it.'

'Sure!' she got up and moved towards her cupboard.

*How did I miss this? What necklace? How will I know which one it is? Where could she have put it?*

She went through Sevita's safe, her jewellery and all her boxes. Kunal watched her search for a good ten minutes.

'Did you forget about it?'

'Of course not. It's just that I can't find it anywhere ...'

'It's been two months. You must have forgotten where you kept it.' He sounded disappointed.

Sama's head buzzed with voices whispering angry words that were beyond her understanding. She didn't want those voices, not with him around. They must go, they must go away!

'I was sure I kept it in the safe. I did!' she said, making her voice quiver a bit. Kunal stood up and walked towards her.

'Hey, it's okay. It will turn up somewhere,' he said. He felt guilty that he had disturbed their peaceful moment. Sama covered her face with her hands.

'It's ... not just that. I feel so hurt ...,' she sighed and leaned on him. He put his arms around her.

'Astha? It will be okay. Give it time.'

'I called her place today. They said she wasn't well and wouldn't be coming to college.'

'Seriously?'

'I'm sure she needs a friend. I won't let what happened to Shruti happen to her. Maybe I should visit her tomorrow, but I don't want to be away from you.'

'Go this Friday. I won't be in town. There's a relative's wedding to attend.'

'You won't be here all day?' she looked into his eyes, anxious.

'Sorry, but I'll have to go,' he said, looking into her big brown eyes.

'Well, all right then,' she said with a smile.

'I guess tonight is one of those nights where I stay with you? The rain makes me think of only you, and how beautiful you are,' he whispered into her ears. He cupped her face in his hands and kissed her, unable to resist her allure.

Sama had managed to distract him from the necklace for now.

—

The next day at college, classes were suspended after lunch because of the heavy rains. The monsoon was at its peak. Astha was absent yet again.

*I wonder what that scum is doing. Calling her dad was fun. I wish I could see what it led to,* Sama thought as she walked out of the class.

That afternoon, Kunal left after dropping her home as he had to go shopping with his mother for the wedding. For once, Sama didn't mind his absence; she had other things to take care of.

Her phone vibrated. It was a message from an unknown number.

*I know you did this, Sevita. You must be happy now, but not for long. I have the screenshots that prove what you did, and they will reach the police.*

Sama snorted and dialled the number. It rang five times before Astha decided to pick up. She was silent.

'I thought you had a lot to say? Why so quiet now?' Sama said in a low voice.

'I can't believe you would stoop so low. You constantly put her down. You made her feel worse than ever. You even let her watch ... '

'How easy it is to blame others. Let her watch what? Can you prove anything?' Sama asked nonchalantly, lying back on her bed.

'I have the screenshots.'

'The screenshots you have mention no names. Who are you talking about?'

Astha was dumbstruck. She hadn't realized it before. The messages Shruti had sent didn't mention either Kunal or Sevita's names.

'You saw the messages on Kunal's phone.'

'Yeah, the messages that show how depressed she was. Also, Astha,' Sama continued, 'the message does say how you didn't help her. How you told her she was overthinking. You say you'll bring the reasons for her death to light, but will you take responsibility for shutting her out?'

'I was there for her, every single time. Just this once, I wasn't. And it's not on me! You have been clawing at her for a long time, and I have seen it,' Astha said, agitated.

'Prove it. What you say has no substance. She could be talking about anyone from the party. It was a big farmhouse, and there were lots of couples around.' Sama dismissed her emotional accusation. 'Stop blaming others. You knew she was depressed, didn't you? Yet, you asked her to enjoy the party. Some friend you are! You stepped away when she needed you the most.'

'I never stepped away—'

'Speaking of stepping away, where have you been for the last two days? Sick?' Her tone changed from cold to icy.

'My mother told you I was sick,' Astha said bitterly, her heart beating faster.

'Oh, and what about before that?'

'That is none of your business!' she snapped. Something in Sevita's tone presaged yet another horror awaiting her. Beads of cold sweat formed on her forehead.

'Well, I'll be in touch. After all, I'm really worried about you. The guilt of Shruti's death must be eating you alive,' Sama said, her tone chilling.

---

Astha's heart beat like crazy after she hung up. What did Sevita know? Did she know about her secret?

'There's no way she knows,' Astha shook her head and murmured to herself. 'I'm just being paranoid. Those screenshots have to be made public even if it affects my reputation. Maybe I can do it anonymously.' She racked her brain. Quickly, she opened her gallery.

Astha carefully blacked her own name out on each of the images. She only had to make it public now and share it with as many people as she could. There was one person who could help her.

'Andrew,' she whispered into her phone.

'Thank god I can hear your voice. Where did you disappear to? What happened to your phone?' He sounded desperate. Astha told him everything that had happened, including her call with Sevita and her fear that she suspected something.

'She doesn't know anything about us. How can she? It's all mind games. But I don't think it's a good idea to meddle anymore. Just let it go,' he told her.

'I can't, not after this. She has gone far enough to blackmail me and get me jailed in my own house. Do you understand my father is already looking for a groom?'

'What?'

'Yes, he said I won't be going back to college. Andrew, if you don't hurry up, he will marry me off.'

'I won't let that happen. Astha, forget about Sevita and other things. Let's just think about us, what we need to do—'

'Andrew, YOU need to think about it. I am a prisoner in my own home.' Warm tears trickled down her face. 'He won't listen to me now. You either persuade him or run away with me. Just do something!'

'I will. Don't worry.'

'Astha!' Her father roared outside her room, knocking angrily. She disconnected the call immediately and hid her iPad under her pillow before sprinting across the room to open the door.

'I was changing, sorry—'

He slapped her before she could finish. 'I saw the CCTV footage of the days you were absent from class. You bitch, where were you?'

A drop of blood rolled out of her nose. She trembled in shock, her head spinning. Her cheek had turned a scorching shade of scarlet. Her father's face was dark with fury. He slapped her again. This time the blood splattered from her nose and her mouth. He continued to thrash her like a madman. Her mother came running upstairs, screaming as she begged her husband to stop.

'She's your daughter! She's our child! Please have mercy, don't beat her anymore!' She grabbed his arm and shielded her from a blow. He finally stopped glaring at the half-unconscious girl. Her mother wrapped her in her arms and wept.

'Ask her where she was. What has she done? Ask her that!' He growled at his wife and left, banging the door hard behind him.

Astha was in a state of mental shock. The physical pain paled in comparison to the sense of hopelessness that gripped her. Her father had always been a chauvinist but had never been violent before. Her half-conscious mind screamed at her to run away with Andrew. Go somewhere far away, out of her father's reach.

She was in no condition to speak or walk the next day. A high fever bound her to her bed. Her worried mother stayed by her side, giving her medicines and praying for her.

Astha was terrified. She would recover one day, and then she would have to face her father again. She would have to answer his questions. It was unthinkable what she had done behind his back, knowing the risk. There was no one she could turn to—Shruti was long gone, while Kunal shunned her. As for Sevita, she wanted her to stay far away.

---

Her fever subsided by nightfall the next day. Astha got up and walked slowly to the bathroom. It was three in the morning, and her parents were asleep. Andrew picked up after a few rings.

'Astha? What's going on?' he asked in a sleepy voice.

'Let's run away,' she said in a weak voice. 'I can't stay here.'

'What's wrong with your voice?'

'I'm … not okay. He beat me. He wants to know where I was …'

'What?' He sat up in horror. 'Tell him you were with Shruti. Ask him to forgive you! You have to convince him.'

'He knows I wasn't with her. I'm locked up. You have to take me away from this place.' Her voice shook. The medicines had done nothing to dull the pain of the beating. Her face, arms and back were swollen with bruises.

'I'm so sorry …'

'Don't be sorry. That won't help. No one can love me like you do. No one cares for me like you do. Let's go. I can't wait any longer.'

Andrew sighed.

'It's not easy to run away like this. I-I'm not prepared. Where will I take you? What will I do? Where will we live?'

'Anywhere will be better than here. I'll work too. Let's just go,' she said.

'Astha ... babe, just hang on for a few months. I'll be done with placements by then—'

'A few months, Andrew? Do you understand that he will marry me off by then?'

'He won't be able to do that so fast, c'mon!'

'You don't know him!'

'It won't happen. Running away is not the solution. We'll figure something out.'

'Figure it out, then. If you want to be with me, that is,' she said bitterly and hung up. She didn't know what to do anymore. Her iPad flashed. Andrew was messaging her, asking her to calm down. He promised that he would find a way out. Despite his assurances, Astha couldn't help but feel hopeless. Then she saw a message from an unknown number.

*Saw your dad in college today. He didn't look happy. Is it about you bunking classes and going off with your friend?*

'Sevita ...' Her breathing became shallow. Another message from the same number only confirmed her worst fears.

*I think I saw what you did.*

---

Two days passed in the same dull stupor. Astha knew she couldn't stretch it much longer. She was unable to sleep at night, jumping up in terror at every sound that indicated her father's movements. All day on Friday, she remained glued to her bed. Her mother had been checking her temperature and bruises regularly without any comment. That evening, however, she spoke to her.

'Your father expects an answer tonight,' she told her softly. Her face was marked by sadness. She held Astha's hands. 'Just ask for forgiveness and do as he says. We have no other way out.'

Once the door was closed behind her, Astha covered her face with her palms, her eyes burning. Was there no way out? Andrew had missed his chance to rescue her, she thought in dismay.

No later than a minute, the doorbell rang. It was four in the afternoon. She could hear her mother's voice in the hall, but couldn't figure out who she was speaking to. She got up and tiptoed out of her room.

'I totally understand. They were such good friends. It makes me sad. Astha must be hurting even more ...'

Astha was aghast when she saw Sevita. She was smiling and holding hands with her mother, comforting her with soothing words, as if they had known each other for ages. Astha knew her worried demeanour was just an act, but she was shocked by how convincing it was.

'My dear, you must be feeling awful yourself,' her mother said as they sat together in the drawing room. Astha could see them from the stairs. 'After going through it all with Sama. I can't imagine how it is for you.'

'That's why I'm really worried. Astha is so sensitive, so delicate inside. I thought I'd come and see her today, maybe try to talk to her. Like I should have done with Sama, or Shruti for that matter.' Her eyes shone with tears as she spoke.

Astha's mother smiled, wiping her own tears, 'Try some Malpua I made. Her father loves them.' She offered Sama the sweets along with a cup of tea. 'Let me tell Astha you are here. I'm sure she would love to see you.'

'Of course!' Sama smiled brightly. Her sweet, well-practised smile worked like a charm on this woman.

Astha was full of trepidation. She swallowed the lump in her throat and walked into the hall.

'Here she is!' Her mother smiled. 'Astha, it's really sweet of Sevita to come visit you. Why don't you girls talk while I get some snacks ready?'

She stood up and gestured to Astha to sit beside Sama before leaving the room. Astha sat upright and stiff as a board, staring at Sama with hatred in her eyes.

---

'Why have you come here? Wasn't it enough for you to call my father?' Astha said scathingly.

'You were not in college for two whole days. I was worried. And is there any particular reason I shouldn't have called your father?' Sama turned to face her, an innocent expression on her face.

'You knew I was bunking classes.'

'But how would I know that? You probably just took leaves. Why do you look so angry?' She shook her head as if in disbelief. 'I don't understand. Did you fall, by the way? There are some bruises on your face.'

Astha shook in anger.

'You know what my father is like. You know what he is capable of when he's angry. And you certainly know I did not fall. Why are you being like this?'

'Why are *you* being like this? What have I ever done to you?' Sama asked her, her voice suddenly cold. Astha shuddered involuntarily. 'Blackmailing me, trying to brainwash Kunal. What is all that?'

'Brainwash? Blackmail? You know what you did, and I have proof,' Astha cried.

'Astha, you are in shock, my friend. The sooner you accept it the better.'

'Shruti killed herself!' Astha nearly screamed.

'Ah, relax, relax. Why don't I show you something fun? You need to enjoy yourself.'

Sama had a lopsided smile as she took out her phone and played a video.

---

The ground beneath Astha's feet moved. Her body broke into a cold sweat. It was Andrew and her, their most intimate moments caught on video.

'How ... how did you do this? How is this possible?' Astha felt dizzy.

'Oh, this?' Sama shrugged. 'It's just a fun video I got from somewhere. Although I do wonder, if I post this online, how viral will it be? People love this sort of stuff.'

'You cannot do that ... don't do that.' Astha's voice was reduced to a whisper. The air wouldn't enter her lungs, and her heart won't stop thudding.

'Why not? It'll be a hit.' Sama leaned closer, her tone turning cold. 'I bet your father watches such stuff in private. He can't be that different from a normal man.'

Astha felt terror in her veins. Sama drew closer to her, her voice dropping, and continued.

'You know, as Shruti's best friend, you did a lousy job. And for whom? This spineless bastard? All he wanted was to fuck you. He hasn't rescued you, has he?' Sama said with a knowing look.

Astha couldn't utter a word.

'By the way, did you know he hasn't stopped doing drugs? He's even dealing in them. If you only knew just how foolish you've been, you'd want to die. Just like Shruti did. Anyway, once this video is online, your father will kill you himself,' Sama said and leaned back on the couch. She took a sip of tea and sighed contentedly.

'You won't leave me alone, will you?'

'Oh no. How can I, Astha? You are the only one left who knows me for who I am. How can I ever stop?' she replied with a smirk.

Astha sat motionless as her mother returned with more snacks. For the next fifteen minutes, she sat still, barely speaking a word. Astha's mother was so desperate for a friend at her daughter's side that she didn't notice anything wrong. When Sama got up to leave, Astha did not say a word to her.

'You don't want to see your friend to the door?' Astha's mother asked her.

'It's okay. I'll show myself out,' Sama said, smiling sweetly. 'Astha, I look forward to seeing you soon. Remember what I said, and take care of yourself. Bye!'

She walked towards the door. Astha's mother accompanied her.

'Aunty, she doesn't seem well at all. I think she is still in shock,' Sama said in an anxious tone, keeping her act immaculate to the very end.

'Yes, but I am glad you came to see her.'

She saw Sama off and came back inside. Astha was walking back to her room.

'You need to talk to your father today. Rest now. We can talk at dinner.'

—

Astha closed the door behind her, standing in silence for a long time. She could hear her mother in the kitchen. Her father would be home soon. Sevita would release the video and life as she knew it would be over. Desperate, she dug her iPad out from under her pillow and called Andrew. He didn't answer. She tried again and was about to give up when he picked up.

'Hi, I'm on my way to Pune. What's going on?'

'Why didn't you take my call? Where were you?'

'Just with some friends. Are you all right?' He sounded like he was in a hurry. Astha could hear a busy road in the background but not the sound of him driving.

'It doesn't sound like you are driving.'

'I've stopped for a bit.'

'Andrew, are you back to dealing drugs?'

'Astha, it is not what you think.'

'You promised me you would stop, and you said you *had* stopped!' Tears streamed down her face.

'I want to take you away from that place. I need to make money to do that.'

'By selling drugs?' she almost yelled at him. 'I thought you had changed, but I was wrong. You had so many days to come and take me away, but you didn't. You don't love me. I was such a fool!'

'Astha, will you relax? It's not—.'

'It doesn't matter anymore. Sevita knows about us and she has a video of us together.'

'What do you mean?' he sounded horrified.

'I mean, there is a video of us having sex in the open,' she said, gritting her teeth.

'How? That's impossible—'

'She will put it online, and my father will come to know.'

Astha broke down, sobbing uncontrollably. She could hear Andrew shouting from the other end, asking her to tell him what exactly had happened. She couldn't speak a word. She felt betrayed and utterly lonely. Astha cut the call, throwing her iPad aside, and hugged her knees as she wept.

---

Astha heard her father parking his car and her mother opening the door. The terror within her intensified. She went into her bathroom and locked herself in. She stared at the door. No matter where she hid, he would break down all the doors and drag her out. Nothing would save her now.

Suddenly, there was a moment of stillness that embraced her. She took a deep breath. It finally dawned on her, a way out, something she hadn't thought was a solution before. It felt peaceful to take a decision of her own at last. Finally, she felt in control.

She removed the blades of a razor and drove one through the veins in her wrists, as deep as she could.

# TIDES TURN

Sama spent a peaceful weekend at home. She spent most of her time on her laptop. Her mother was home, but she avoided her. She told her she had a lot of homework and didn't venture into the living room.

Kunal returned on Saturday and came over at night. She told him how happy Astha had been to see her and how ill she had looked because of the fever. She told him that she thought Shruti's death had affected Astha badly. Kunal hugged and comforted her.

Monday came quickly. Black clouds were gathering, indicating a stormy day ahead. Sama wondered if Astha had taken her advice and killed herself. As she strolled through the parking lot and down the corridors with Kunal, she noticed that no policemen were around.

*Maybe that scum didn't do it. Well, as long as she can keep her mouth shut ...*

---

The sky roared, and it rained. While she was sitting in the canteen at lunch, Sama got a call from an unknown number. Kunal was at the vending machine.

'Hello?'

'Sevita,' said a man's voice, husky with anger.

'Who's this?'

'You will come to know who I am very soon. Come to the parking lot.'

'Don't call me again or I'll report you to the police.'

'And so will I.'

She frowned.

'You did this to her. You did this to Astha. I don't know how, not yet, but I will find out, and I will hunt you down.'

'Yeah? Let me see you try. Your baseless claims can't touch me. And anyway, I have no clue what you are talking about.'

'That's clever. No loose ends anywhere. But how long can you keep this up?'

The guy hung up. She stared at the phone. That could only have been ...

*Andrew. But what has that bitch gone and done?*

Later, when Sama was walking towards the parking lot with Kunal, she saw a shadow lurking behind a tree.

'Kunal, wait for me here? I'll get a cold drink.'

'Sure, all good?'

'Yes, of course. I'm just thirsty.' She stood on her toes and planted a kiss on his cheek. 'I'll come soon.'

Kunal smiled and walked towards his car. Sama swiftly hid behind the nearest vehicle and watched Andrew look around. He didn't approach Kunal. Clearly, he was waiting for her. After a while, he gave up and walked away. She had avoided being cornered by him. But she could feel a thousand needles under her skin. What was he trying to do?

*Another piece of scum. I will not let him interfere ...*

As it didn't rain heavily the next day, the college remained open, and classes were held as usual. Sama felt uneasy whenever she thought of Andrew. Was he still lurking around? Was he watching her? She had received ten missed calls from his number yesterday. She tapped her pencil impatiently as she waited for the lectures to be over. Maybe she shouldn't go with Kunal towards the parking lot at all. He was sure to be waiting there. The mystery of what had happened to Astha was adding to her agitation.

There was no word about her, online or anywhere else. Of course, Astha's dad was a big shot, more than capable of making news disappear. His pride was the size of a mountain. What was he hiding, though? Her hands were becoming sweaty.

'You don't look well.'

She snapped out of her thoughts when Kunal came up to her. It was lunchtime already.

'It's the weather, I guess.'

'Hmm, what do you say we go to your place? No one's there today, right?' He smiled. Sama's anxious thoughts momentarily vanished.

'Yeah! I'll order some food. Wait for me outside the gate?'

'Why don't you walk with me?' he said, confused.

'I need to use the washroom,' she said with a laugh.

---

They spent the rest of the day together in her living room, eating pizza and watching movies. In the evening, Sama laid out a picnic mat on the lawn. She sat on his lap, pulling his hands inside her blouse.

'Neighbours!' he whispered, chuckling.

'They can't see the lawn. Besides, they don't come back till eight.'

'You've done your research ...'

'Yeah, because I've been wanting to do this for a long time.' She kissed him and played with his hair.

'There's something I've been wanting to do as well.' He picked her up, making her gasp. Then he carried her all the way to the living room and put her gently on the couch, gazing into her mysterious eyes.

---

The next day, Sama seemed to be glowing. She had cooked a special lunch for the two of them. It seemed a romantic idea to have a picnic meal, away from the college crowd. They walked to the edge of the campus, hand in hand, enjoying the beautiful weather.

'Hi there, Sevita!'

Sama froze. She turned around slowly, as did Kunal. Andrew was walking towards them with a weird grin. His eyes were red.

'Who are you?' she asked, sounding surprised.

'Oh? Well played,' he said, watching her clutch Kunal's arm. 'Should I remind you?'

'Back off, mate. She doesn't know you.' Kunal stepped forward and put an arm across her.

'Is this the way you want to do it?' Andrew said. 'I did try to talk to you in a reasonable way, but you played tough, remember?'

'What the hell are you saying? We have never met, and I don't know you,' she said angrily, still holding Kunal's arm.

'That's it. You get away from us now!' Kunal warned him.

'All right then,' Andrew said. 'You don't know what you are getting into, do you? No problem, she knows where to find me.' He waved a bony hand and walked away, his face smug.

'Kunal, who was that crazy man?' she said, her eyebrows arched in anxiety.

'Hell if I know. Let's go back. It's not safe with such weirdos around. He seemed high on something.'

Kunal led her towards the canteen area. It had been a strange encounter, but with everything happening around them lately, nothing surprised him anymore.

Despite herself, Sama was shaken.

*He spoilt my lunch date. He will regret this.*

---

That night, she turned on the live footage from the CCTV camera she had installed in the abandoned house. For the third night in a row, Andrew was sitting there, huddled next to a small campfire. A pile of cigarette butts and a pocket-knife lay by his side. He was wearing headphones and a furious look on his face. He sat waiting for Sama, smoking one cigarette after another, impatient with every minute that passed in futility.

Sama decided to put an end to this. She put on a silky kimono and climbed out of her room through her window. She followed the familiar trail into the woods with just a small torch in her hand. The rain had abated, and the sky seemed to be asleep as the clouds floated across in grey masses. A half-moon hung on the horizon, making the woods glimmer in silvery light. She reached the house and stood at the gate. Andrew's bloodshot eyes fell on her. His lips were set in a grim line. He took his headphones off and got up.

'You look lost,' Sama said.

'Shut up, you bitch. I will cut you up and make sure no one finds your body ... like your sister's. Then we'll talk about who's lost ...'

He flashed open the pocketknife and walked threateningly towards her. She watched him take long strides that covered the distance between them. Her lips curved into a smile.

'Impressive.' She let the torch fall on the ground and gazed into his eyes. He blinked in surprise. 'I see why she fell for you,' Sama said as she pulled a string around her waist and shrugged the kimono off her shoulder. 'That protective nature, superficial as it is, was her only hope ...'

He stopped in his tracks, speechless. Her bare arms seemed to glimmer in the silver light. Her white, lacy sleepwear revealed her curves. His eyes fell on her chest, as it rose up and down with her breathing. He could almost see through the thin layer of the garment. She put one foot in front of the other elegantly as she closed the distance between them, slowly, suggestively, until her body almost touched his. He looked into her eyes, spellbound. His heart raced.

'I know what you want. What you need,' she whispered softly and leaned towards him, her lips closer to his ear. 'You are angry only because you think you can't have it anymore ...' Her fingers glided across his arm, knocking the pocket knife out of his hand. She looked up at him once again. His anger had been completely defused.

'Now, stop with this act of caring about her.' Her smile suddenly vanished, and her tone dropped menacingly low. He felt his blood curdle with a strange fear as he looked into her eyes. How did they turn from seductive to terrifying so quickly? How could she take him from a state of arousal to one of fear in a matter of seconds?

'Neither of you loved each other. It was just an escape from your drab reality ... and some physical pleasure. But I guess you know that, right? You wouldn't lust after another woman if you loved her. You wouldn't make false promises.'

Andrew was covered in cold sweat. How did she know so much?

Almost as if she knew what he was thinking, she added, 'I know all about you, and I have proof. Stay away from me.' She picked up her kimono and the torch. 'I hope never to see you again, Andrew. Goodbye.'

Andrew was rooted to the spot as he watched her go. He didn't know for how long he stood there. When his fear dissolved and he started to breathe again, he doubled over and fell to his knees.

'What have I done?' he said to himself in disbelief. He curled his palms into fists, embarrassed and frustrated with himself. 'I love Astha. I love her. But I couldn't show it ...'

He sobbed hopelessly. Astha had trusted him with her life, but he couldn't rescue her in time. And now, he had lost all control over himself. He tore his hair, punishing himself as he wept, lying curled up on the ground. Clouds covered the moon, and the woods fell into the embrace of darkness, as did his heart. With the darkness came a grim calm. He wouldn't give up just yet.

'I will expose her. Somehow I will. One day, she's bound to slip.' He lay on the ground and stared at the dark sky. 'I will not let her get away with what she has done.'

---

The whispers about Astha started the next day. Someone's father was a doctor, and he had come to know what had happened to the daughter of Lavasa's most influential politician.

'She seems to have been in the ICU,' a girl was telling everyone before the class began. Kunal shook his head sadly. What was happening to his friends? Yet again, he hadn't seen it coming. Sama was listening to the girl, wide-eyed with shock.

'It looks like she attempted suicide,' the girl said in hushed tones.

'Is it because of Shruti?' someone else asked.

'I can't say. But it's like a curse is spreading in this town. Guys, we should start a support group. It is happening again and again to people in our very own class! We must listen to these silent cries for help and reach out to those in need.'

Sama's attention drifted away from the girl's useless speech.

*Attempted?! That worthless piece of trash! Why didn't she die? And why was that spineless boyfriend of hers after me if she's still alive? How stupid!*

'Sevita...?' She snapped out of her trance and looked up. It was Kunal and he looked deathly pale.

'I think, we should visit her.'

'Of course ...'

The muffled voices in her head had started to scream and wail again. Astha had to be silenced. Completely.

# SLENDERMAN

Kunal and Sevita left before the classes began. As he drove to the hospital, Kunal was consumed with regret. Sama put on a worried expression, but she was raging inside. Why was he so easily affected by everything around him? Why did he care so much? She couldn't understand it.

They reached the hospital. Astha's mother was sitting outside the ICU, her face pale and her eyes sunken. She greeted Sama and Kunal with a wan smile. Her daughter had caring friends, she thought, and maybe their visit would comfort her.

'How did you come to know about this? I'm so glad you did, though.' Her eyes filled with tears. 'Maybe she will feel better after seeing you and want to live again,' she said before sobs overtook her. Kunal didn't know how to react. Sama smiled sadly, her eyes moist.

'Don't worry, it'll be all right,' she comforted Astha's mother and went inside the ICU ward with Kunal. Astha lay unconscious. Her wrists were bandaged heavily. Drips were needled into her veins. The sight disturbed Kunal.

'I'll wait for you outside,' he said and left. Sama sat beside her, watching her face and listening to the beeps from the heart monitor. After a few minutes, Astha's eyes fluttered open, staring at the door in front of her in a semi-conscious state.

'You know, I so badly want to kill you right now. I could pull a needle or that mask away, even poison you, but you won't suffer as much as I want you to.' The heart monitor beeped at closer intervals. Astha seemed to recognize her voice. 'You didn't cut your veins deep enough, you moron.' She trailed her finger across the bandaged wrist. Astha's breathing became erratic. She couldn't move or speak.

'Relax, I won't kill you right now. However, you should know by now that I won't hesitate to make those recordings public. Your father already suspects you. Oh, and also, no one cares about you.' She leaned closer and locked Astha's eyes in an unfeeling stare. 'Once you are out of here. I wonder what will happen to you.'

Astha's eyes were wide with terror, and her body shook. The heart monitor beeped frantically. Sama stood up calmly and, with one last look of warning, walked out.

'I think she needs rest. She's still unconscious,' she told Astha's mom as she closed the door behind her.

'Thanks for coming to see her.'

'I'll visit again.'

'Some faces I recognize are here!' Mohite's ringing baritone dulled Sama's smile. He was the last person on earth she wanted to see. Why was he there?

'Inspector Mohite,' she stood up to face him with a formal smile and shook hands with him despite herself. 'How are you?'

'I'm good, but it seems like things in this town are not,' he said. His eyes were as piercing as she remembered. She swallowed.

Once again, he seemed to be scanning not only her movements but her very thoughts. She composed herself and let out a small sigh full of apprehension, looking down at the floor. Meeting his eyes was like playing with fire.

'Ma'am, would you ask your husband to come here once you reach home? I have a few things to discuss.'

'Sure ...'

'Kunal, you should escort her outside,' commanded the inspector. 'She hasn't slept for several nights in a row. Don't worry, ma'am, the hospital staff will take care of Astha.'

Kunal sprang up to escort Astha's mother to her car. They were soon out of sight.

'Mind if I smoke?'

'You can't smoke in here.'

'Of course not. Let's go to the balcony.' His eyes were still fixed on her.

'I don't smoke. Please carry on.' She confronted his piercing look with a calculated smile.

'Let's get to the point then. Sevita, you're the last person, besides her mother, whom Astha met before attempting suicide. Care to tell me what that meeting was about?'

'I'm sorry, but is this an interrogation?'

'I can make it one if that gets you talking. Would you want that?'

Her jaws clenched. When he gestured towards the balcony, she had to follow against her will.

'So,' he asked as he lit his Cuban cigar, 'what did you two talk about?'

'Her absence from college after Shruti's death. She said she was in shock and was running a fever.'

'What did you say?' He took a puff and watched her like a hawk. She was calm on the surface but furious inside.

There was cold reluctance in her tone. It was clear she didn't like him a bit.

'Everything I could. I told her things would be okay. That I miss her in college, and that I am always there for her.'

'In short, all the things you couldn't say to Shruti.'

'Kind of. But it didn't really help. What has to happen, happens,' she said, sounding resigned. Mohite watched her as he smoked. Sometimes, it was almost as if her body contradicted her tone, yet she managed to convince most people that she was sincere. Mohite was not so sure.

'Did you notice anything odd about Astha that day?'

'Yeah, a lot of things were odd,' Sama said. She shook her head slightly as if trying to remember. 'She had what looked like bruises on her face. I even asked her about them. And it was odd the way she seemed so scared. I don't know what to say. Astha didn't tell me anything else,' she said, looking away from the inspector. The clouds were starting to gather again. 'Looks like it will rain.'

'Yes, a storm is brewing. It may hit Lavasa.' He watched her from the corner of his eyes as he puffed on his cigar. 'Do you know if she was involved with anyone outside college?'

Sama snorted.

'Her father would've killed her if she'd ever done something like that. It was always home to college and back for her. She wasn't even allowed to watch a movie with friends. Only when her father was not home and her mother covered for her could she come with us. There's no way she could be involved with an outsider. Why are you asking this? I'm sure you know what a big shot her father is.'

*Careful. Don't give him any information that he doesn't ask for*, said a raspy voice in her head.

'Yes, I do. But so should you. I wonder why you called him and not her mother to ask about her well-being.'

Sama felt her heart knock against her ribs. He knew every detail, didn't he?

'Does it matter? Big shot or not, he would know how his daughter is doing. Besides, it's easier to find his office number online. I didn't have her mother's.' She shrugged, brushing the question off as if it were silly.

'I see,' Mohite said, looking away into the clouds.

Once again, he was stuck. Why had Astha attempted suicide? The bruises had been reported by the doctor, and they had not been caused by a fall. She didn't seem to have any connections outside her family and college, though he was still keeping that line of inquiry open. He knew about her father wanting the CCTV footage from college, too, as he had spoken to the principal.

'You should get home soon. It will rain heavily anytime now,' he said.

'It's only fat clouds and no rain, really. I bet it'll just be a slight drizzle.'

'Let's not underestimate them based on the way they look now.'

She glanced at him. He was still looking at the clouds clustering together in the sky.

'Well then, have a good day,' Sama said and walked off. The inspector followed her after putting his cigar out. Astha's father was waiting for him in the corridor. Sama and Kunal hastily took their leave.

As she drove back to college with Kunal, Sama continued to stare at the clouds.

*He's like those clouds I should not underestimate. Even if there is nothing that connects me to these events, I need to be on my toes.*

She felt disturbed after her conversation with Mohite. If he ever discovered something to link her to these deaths, it would mean trouble for her. She wished she had stabbed Andrew when she had the chance. No one would have noticed his absence besides his customers. And she would have successfully eliminated one loose end.

---

'Sir, this is really beyond our reach,' Gadre said as he handed the report over to his boss. It was only noon, but clouds had swallowed the sun, and it was almost dark when Inspector Mohite reached the police station.

'Why? Because he's a politician?' Mohite glared at Gadre, who grinned nervously.

'He is the biggest politician in Lavasa, sir!'

'Doesn't mean he can get away with domestic abuse. The medical reports are clear and unquestionable.'

'Yes, but sir, he is taking his daughter to Mumbai for treatment. He's leaving his campaign for the coming elections to be with her.'

'None of that means he should not be punished for beating her black and blue. I won't let him off that easy.'

'As you wish, sir. But I think he's learnt his lesson already. Do you know his daughter has stopped talking?'

Mohite looked at him with a frown, waiting for details. Gadre continued. 'I have a friend. One of the security personnel her father's hired to guard her ward. He told me the girl is unable to speak and goes berserk if anyone asks her questions.'

'What sort of questions?'

'Like what happened the day she attempted suicide. When they asked her about her absence from college, she panicked and fainted. Her blood pressure sank so low that they shifted her back to the ICU. Now the doctor has restricted every outsider except her mother from entering the ward.'

'Even the father is forbidden to enter?'

'Yes, she seemed frightened when he came in to see her. What a sad feeling for a father,' Gadre said.

Mohite was intrigued. 'What happened that day, I wonder, besides her meeting Sevita.'

'So you still think she's connected to all this, sir?' Gadre looked astonished.

'Yet another person she was close to tried to kill themselves. It doesn't strike you as odd?'

'Yes, third girl in a matter of almost three months,' Gadre admitted.

'Don't forget the boy who died in the freak accident.'

'But that was not a suicide, sir,' Gadre reminded him.

'No, but the way it happened ... something was odd. However, there's no evidence,' Mohite said. 'But the next time this happens, I'll have proof.'

'Next time?' Gadre almost shrieked in alarm. 'You think there will be a next time, sir?'

'It's a hunch ...' Mohite stared at the wall of his office, puffing at his cigar. He hoped and prayed that his hunch was wrong.

---

Kunal dropped Sama home and left early. She began checking the day's footage from the woods. Andrew had not been there all day. Where was he now? Had he given up and gone back?

*He must have. What else could scum like him do?*

She got up early the next morning and made herself a cup of coffee. It looked like a clear day; there were fewer clouds in the sky. Birds sang as the sun rose sluggishly. She sat on a swing in the garden and sipped her coffee.

Suddenly Sama tensed up. There was someone on the hills facing her back garden who seemed to be watching her. She put her cup down on the patio table and quickly used the zoom option on her phone's camera to take a picture. She looked at it, but there was no one in the frame.

Had she imagined it? She took her cup and went back inside.

'You look grumpy,' her mother remarked. She had heard about what happened with Astha from a friend and was worried for her daughter.

'I'm not. I'm getting late,' she said and brushed past her mother to her room. Had someone been watching her? Could Andrew be hiding amongst the trees somewhere across her house? It was an unsettling feeling.

Kunal picked her up as usual, and they drove to their college. She was distant, the figure on the hill still on her mind.

'Hey, I was telling you about the pictures I got from the wedding photographer.'

'Yes, I'm all ears. I want to see them soon. Send them to me?'

'Yup, if you can handle my hotness,' he joked. Later that day, Kunal noticed that she seemed to flinch slightly every time she looked over her shoulder or in the direction of the hills. He asked her if she was okay, and she simply nodded with a smile.

How could Sama tell him? She was sure she had seen Andrew hiding behind a tree as they arrived in the parking lot, then standing on a hill as they walked towards the canteen, and in many other corners. He was following her, and it was no illusion.

Confronting him was not an option now that the police were involved in Astha's case.

*What should I do with him?*

---

Sama tossed and turned in her bed that night. She had made sure to cover her windows with a double layer of curtains. But how long could she hide from him? He was following her like a shadow.

Her phone rang. An unknown number was calling her. She knew who it was. Taking a deep breath, she picked up. No words were spoken for several seconds.

'I am watching you. You know that. I can see your room's light switched on.'

It was Andrew's voice. He sounded like he was high. Was he doing drugs again? She wished he would overdose and die.

'You made Astha want to kill herself. You made her do it. I know that for sure. I will avenge her, just you see.'

Sama didn't speak a word.

Andrew continued, 'You cannot harm her anymore. She was shifted out of Lavasa last night.' Sama blinked in surprise. He went on, 'Now you cannot visit her. I know you went to the hospital yesterday. You mocked my feelings for her, and now I don't care about any leverage you may have. You've already done much worse. I'll happily go to jail if that exposes you. I will follow you all the way to hell. I will keep watching you till one day you slip—'

Sama hung up and blocked the number. The voices in her head got louder. They screamed, and they shrieked in agony. Acid from her gut seemed to spread.

*Pay ... make him pay ... you will be found out ... Kunal will know ... Astha will tell on you ... Andrew will break in and kill you ... he's watching ... he's not scared anymore ... he's lost everything, and now you have everything to lose!*

A sharp pain almost split her head in two. She groaned. The voices were whispering and shouting, screaming and weeping. It was worse than ever. The walls seemed to have eyes, and the bed seemed to breed monsters. All the furniture in the room seemed to close in on her, shrieking with contorted faces.

'Stop ... stop, stop, STOP!' She muffled her voice with a cushion. Her hands twitched. She wanted her insects back.

It seemed like the night would never end. She couldn't sleep, and she couldn't stop the voices. All she could do was curl up on her bed and clasp her head in her hands.

# CACOPHONY

Sama sat in the living room, her face devoid of expression. She was still dizzy after the night's ordeal. The voices in her head were quieter, but they hadn't stopped. Nasty little whispers echoed inside, scratching her brain.

There was a prickly feeling on her back as if Andrew's eyes were staring a hole in it. She had received many more messages from him, from other unknown numbers, threatening to ruin her life. He had called her several times.

It was 7.45 a.m. She was waiting for Kunal. Her breakfast lay untouched. Her eyes were sunken and slightly red. Mrs Vyas watched her sit there like she was set in stone. Her husband had left for work early. She sighed, wondering how to start a conversation with her daughter. Since when had it become so tough to talk to her?

'It must've been difficult to see Astha like that. How is her mother doing?' she asked, choosing her words carefully.

'Not well,' Sama answered without a hint of emotion. 'She had stayed awake for days to look after her...'

A strange sensation came over her without warning as she spoke those words. Something had been preying on her soul ever since she had met Astha's mom in the ICU. The look of worry on her face, her tears ... It had been strangely touching.

'She really cares about Astha. She did everything possible to save her.'

'Well, that's no surprise. It's what mothers do, my dear. I'd do the same for you,' Mrs Vyas said. Her hands shook as she imagined Sevita in Astha's situation. Mrs Vyas took a deep breath and dismissed the thought. She continued carving a huge watermelon on the kitchen counter. Other fruits were arranged on a plate next to it, ready to be decorated with cream, cherries and a homemade honey syrup.

'Tell me, Maa ...'

'Tell you what?'

'If Sama was found,' she began, holding the cup of coffee in her hand, 'if she was found and hospitalized like that, would you have looked after her?'

Her mother looked at her, shocked. 'What a question, Sevita. Of course, I would've. Why wouldn't I?'

'Well, because you never loved her. Not that I could see ...'

Mrs Vyas sighed. They had never spoken about Sama and their feelings about her suicide. She should have done this earlier.

'I did love her. She was my daughter, just like you are. It was ... just a bit different with her. Sama herself was different.'

'Different how?' she asked, swishing the coffee in the cup. 'I think she was smart. Introverted, but really smart.'

'Yeah, she was always a straight-A student in school. It wasn't about her smartness. It was just the way she was. You know that. You realized it too.'

'I realized she was uninterested in the things we were into. Things like mingling with people who were not as intelligent, or having regular hobbies that anyone might have ...'

'That did make it uncomfortable for us all, right? Sama was difficult to raise. She could never mix in a crowd or make friends. She stood out too much, not to say that was a bad thing. Sometimes she was just strange.'

'Strange? Like on the day that puppy died?'

'Yeah ...' Her mother let out a shaky breath. 'And the day I saw her kill the insects she was hiding. I know you and your father thought I was being too strict, but the look in her eyes was frightening. It was not right,' Mrs Vyas said as she shook her head. She continued to carve the watermelon in a neat, geometrical pattern all the while.

'The look in her eyes?' Sama repeated. The coffee was cold now.

'Didn't you ever notice? She had a strange way of looking at people. I never could say what she was thinking. She looked at me like that too, as if I was an object. As a mother, I didn't feel great about it.'

'You could've changed it, right, if she was still alive?'

Mrs Vyas remained silent for some time.

'No, I don't think so. I couldn't do anything all those years she was growing up. I doubt I would be able to now. She would have just gotten worse with time. Maybe what she did was right.'

Sama set the coffee cup down.

Mrs Vyas continued, 'Maybe that was the only way for her, and she knew it. A normal life was impossible for her. It's sad but true.'

Sama stood up and walked to the kitchen with her cup. She placed it in the microwave and set it for half a minute.

'So, you think it's a good thing that she died?' she asked, watching the cup spin inside the microwave. Her mind was suddenly blank, her hands limp.

'I would never say that. But she wasn't capable of living

a happy life. What happened was probably the only way. Anyhow, no point in thinking about it.'

Sama turned to look at her mother. She watched her bend over the watermelon. Mrs Vyas moved the knife in a zig-zag pattern, carving its edges carefully.

The silvery glare of the knife's blade fell on her face.

A sudden rush came over Sama. She advanced fiercely and pushed her mother's elbow hard. Instead of the fruit, the knife cut into her throat and pierced her vocal cords with its sharpened edge.

---

Mrs Vyas stumbled, clutching her neck. Strange noises came from her throat as she tried to scream for help. Slowly, she turned towards her daughter, her eyes wide with shock. Sama had stepped away neatly before the pool of her mother's blood could touch her. Her palms and face felt hot, but her mind was calm. The voices were gone. She felt clearheaded, lively almost.

Mrs Vyas fell on the floor. Shaking all over, voiceless, she tried to crawl out of the kitchen. Sama watched her as if she was an injured insect trying to escape. The corner of her lip curled in a lopsided smile, and her neck bent to her right as she looked at her mother struggle, spitting blood all over the white marble floor.

'That puppy was annoying,' she said casually. 'Sevita would play with it all the time. You would feed it milk and bread. Pet it and play with it. I used to feel as if the two of you preferred that filthy animal over me. And it was true. You proved that today.'

Mrs Vyas looked at her daughter, confused. She was losing a lot of blood and had trouble focusing. When her eyes fell on her daughter, she saw the same expression she had seen so many times before. The same look Sama used to have when she killed those insects.

The truth finally dawned on her.

She realized what it meant and what had really happened on the bridge. She tried to crawl faster into the hall. Sama walked backwards slowly, letting her writhe in pure agony.

'You look just like that puppy now, leaving a trail of blood behind as you try to save your sorry existence. I'll let you in on a secret. I beat that puppy and broke its limbs, with the very plate you always fed it from, and threw it on the road.'

Mrs Vyas's phone was kept on the centre table next to the TV. She struggled to reach it as life ebbed out of her.

'Can't reach it?' Sama pulled the table away from her. 'Anyway, it's not like you can speak now, is it?'

Mrs Vyas was losing consciousness. There was blood all over. Her saree was soaked too. Her breath came out in wheezing gasps of anguish as her windpipe and lungs filled with blood.

'Well then, Maa, it looks like it's almost time for me to leave, or I'll be late for college. Don't wait up for me; I'll be late today,' Sama said, picking up her bag. She looked into the almost lifeless gaze of the woman who was her mother one last time and walked out, closing the door behind her.

---

'Bye, Maa! I'm off!' she shouted cheerfully as she walked across the front lawn. Her neighbour smiled at her, and she returned the smile with a wave. A minute later, Kunal arrived. She wished him good morning with a deep kiss.

'Wow, your mood has improved!'

'Yes. I had a great conversation with Maa today ... for the first time after ... you know. And I think that was just what I needed!' She strapped her seat belt on and flashed a brilliant smile at him. The corner of his eyes crinkled as he returned the smile and ruffled her hair.

'I'm happy to see you happy.'

'Yeah? Then it's up to you to make me even happier! I feel like going for a drive and spending the whole day with you, what say?'

'Well, most of the classes are cancelled anyway, so why not? I think we can afford to go for a long, long drive today.'

---

Mohan Vyas was sitting by the dam as his team measured water levels. The approaching storm had put the engineers on alert. They analysed the structure for possible failures and cracks, as heavy rains had filled it almost to the brim. A storm was approaching, and they were on alert. They would have to open the gates of the dam that day.

As he supervised the process, Mr Vyas fought to keep thoughts of his dead daughter at bay. Since her death, he had thrown himself into his work, but he had not stopped thinking of her for a single day. She had always been different. He had loved her dearly, and his heart ached when he remembered her shy smile. He had failed as a father. He had failed as a responsible adult. His heart was in pieces, and yet his wife seemed to have overcome the ordeal pretty easily. He despised her for going back to her hobbies and the routines of normal life in no time. In fact, he avoided spending time with her for this reason. He struggled with the reality of Sama's loss every day and kept asking why it had happened.

It took a hard day's work to pull everything off smoothly. The team celebrated in the evening. They had handled dangerous water levels in the dam without any casualties, among civilians or employees. Mr Vyas felt drained and exhausted. After drinking a cup of tea with his colleagues, he left for his house. His driver opened the gate and drove into the compound. Mr Vyas told him to leave for the day and rang the doorbell.

No answer. 'Strange...' He rang the bell again. No one answered the door. The house was unusually silent. Normally, the TV would be switched on, or his wife would be on the phone in the kitchen, taking orders. He could always hear her voice from where he stood on the doorstep. Today, it was eerily quiet. He pushed the door, and it swung open. It was not locked from the inside. An ominous feeling drenched him in a cold sweat. It was pitch dark inside. He switched the lights on as he entered the living room.

'Sevita? Shilpa?' He called out, but no one answered. He took his coat off and threw it on the sofa, frowning and looking around. It was only when he sat down on the couch in the living room to take his socks off that he saw the sight. He screamed at the top of his lungs. His driver, who was still at the gate, came running back inside and screamed in his turn when he entered the house. Mrs Shilpa Vyas's lifeless body lay in a pool of blood.

---

Sama watched Kunal as he drove towards her house. They had spent a long and beautiful day together. The silhouette of his face as he drove, his twinkling eyes when he glanced at her, his shoulders ... she wanted all of it. Yet, that night, she knew she wouldn't be able to sleep with him. Something terrible was waiting for her back home. She was prepared for it.

'What is going on?' Kunal frowned when he saw a number of police cars outside her gate and an ambulance parked inside.

'Why are all these people here?' She looked at him, her face pale. They rushed out of the car. The front door was open. She burst into the house.

'No!' she screamed and fell on her knees, covering her mouth. Kunal stood petrified. The bloodied corpse of Sama's mother lay on the floor. There was a boundary drawn around her and 'Do Not Cross' tapes everywhere.

'Maa!' Sama wailed and sobbed, clutching her hair and shaking all over. A woman kneeled by her side and tried to comfort her. Sama's eyes fell on the floor next to her mother, which the police had marked off. A chill ran down her spine when she saw it; she had to hide her surprise. Sama had known what she would come home to that night, but she didn't expect to see her own name written in blood all over the white marble floor. Her mother had written 'SAMA' on the floor in her own blood.

---

*That woman hated me till the last moment of her life. She wants to tell everyone who killed her. I won't let that happen.*

Kunal kneeled at her side, unable to react. Sama's dad sat, almost lifeless, on the couch. His driver had covered him with a shawl and was rubbing his shoulders.

'Make sure all the evidence is carefully tagged,' she heard a voice say.

Sama flinched. It was Inspector Mohite. Was her facade good enough? She had to be very careful.

'She did this because of Sama,' she sobbed. 'She said how sorry she was in the morning. I thought she was opening up, but I was wrong. Once again, once again I failed!' She leaned on Kunal's shoulder, pouring her heart out. He helped her get up, and they followed the inspector outside. With everything Kunal had seen over the past weeks, he was traumatized. He sat with her in the garden, caressing her head and muttering, 'It will be all right,' as if to calm himself.

The hours dragged by. It was almost midnight. Mohite waited patiently for the forensic team to wind up their initial examination of the scene. Mr Vyas had been taken to the hospital after his blood pressure had plummeted.

The inspector stood in a corner, his hands deep in the pockets of his suede coat with wide lapels as he surveyed the scene. Gadre was also around. He glanced at his boss from time to time, looking scared. Mohite had predicted another tragedy, and, to his horror, it had turned out to be true.

Inspector Mohite stepped into the garden and lit a particularly large Cuban cigar. This case had pushed him to the edge. The brutality of Mrs Vyas's murder was uncommon; he believed it was murder, not suicide. He imagined her crawling on the floor, trying to reach her phone, unable to utter a single word. All she could do was write one word on the floor with her own blood. And she had written her dead daughter's name. What could she have meant? He finished the cigar and walked towards the wrought-iron table and chairs on the front lawn. Kunal was sitting there next to Sama and rubbing her back. To all appearances, she was exhausted from weeping and grieving for her mother.

'Kunal, you should go back home. Let one of my men escort you,' he said. Kunal looked up at him, hesitating. 'Don't worry about her. She needs some medical attention. I plan to take her to her father and make sure she sleeps under a doctor's observation. The shock could affect her health if she doesn't get some rest soon.'

'No ... please ... I don't want to go anywhere. Kunal, please stay!'

'Sorry, Sevita, but I need some answers right now. This is an official investigation I'm heading, and this is how I'll do it.'

Sama looked up with tearful eyes only to meet his sharp gaze. A constable appeared to escort Kunal home. He was half-relieved, and half-worried for Sevita. However, he had no choice but to leave.

Inspector Mohite took out yet another cigar.

'I'll need this today,' he said as he lit a dark brown roll of fine tobacco. He pushed the striker on a lighter and lit the cigar. Tobacco burnt bright in scarlet. He pocketed the lighter and sat on an iron chair, taking a deep breath. A silence fell between them as he took one drag after another. Sama let out weak sobs at intervals, hugging herself as if she was cold. A soft light from a garden lamp lit the lawn. It was hard for them to see each other's faces, but Mohite no longer needed to look at her face in order to observe her.

'What happened in the morning?' he asked coolly.

'I-I got ready early ... and I was sitting in the living room. She was making fruit salad for an order. That's her hobby ... was her hobby.' She did not look at him as she spoke. 'I left a little before eight. I said bye to her. I didn't know it was forever,' Sama said, her voice teary.

'What did you two talk about? You said something before ...'

'She asked me how Astha and her mother were doing. You know I had gone to see them. She was sad about what had happened. Then the topic switched to Sama. She asked me how I would have felt if we had found Sama. She said she would have taken care of her just like Astha's mom is caring for Astha.'

'And ...?'

'And I thought she was opening up about Sama's death. She had not talked about it since that day. I felt relieved when she finally did. I came to know what was in her heart, at last.'

'What do you mean?'

'Just that on the surface she looked okay, but I had heard her sob when dad was away, working. He hasn't been there a lot after Sama. She had no one but me, and I was too weak to support her. Things have been really, really bad since Sama's death. It was Shruti next, and then Astha.' Fat tears rolled down her cheeks. 'I only ever wanted to listen to Mom, so I did. She wished Sama's body could be found at least ... that she could've done more for her ... loved her more ...'

'Loved her more?'

'Sama was different. No one could ever get very close to her emotionally. Mom believed if she had tried a bit more, maybe that would have made a difference.'

'Isn't that what you also said about yourself?'

'Yes, we all believe it. My father too. I'm scared what he will do ...' She covered her face and wept. 'I have no one but him ... I don't want to be an orphan!'

Inspector Mohite took a few more drags and let her sob. Sama stopped after a while. It wasn't working.

'You were sitting in the living room, you said. Where exactly?'

'On the couch.'

'What were you doing at the time?'

'I was having my breakfast.'

'What did you have?'

'Eggs, toast and coffee. Why is that relevant?'

'Did you eat your eggs and toast?'

'I … I couldn't. Mom started talking about Sama, and I lost my appetite.'

'So how do you think your mother died?'

---

A chill went down her spine.

'Don't ask me such things. There was so much blood. I don't want to think about it.'

'You think it could have been a freak accident while she was carving the melon?'

'I don't know. I just don't know. There was too much blood!' She clutched her hair and shook her head.

'You think she could have cut her wrists?'

'What will you accomplish by asking me the same thing over and over again?' she sobbed loudly, drawing attention from a few onlookers. Mohite ignored it.

'You think a person can commit suicide by cutting their own throat?'

'I don't know! Maybe it was a freak accident. Maybe it was intentional … I don't know.'

'Why did she write "Sama"?'

'Why? I told you why … she was feeling bad about what had happened, and somehow I think she must've blamed herself. What other reason could there be?'

'Why not "sorry"?'

'I don't know!'

'If she intended to kill herself, wouldn't she at least have sent a message to someone?'

She shuddered inwardly. Why was he talking about messages? Did he by any chance find out about Shruti's messages?'

'Inspector, I don't know! She had a mind of her own and did what she wanted to do!'

'Do you think the force with which her throat was stabbed could have been self-inflicted?'

'What?' She was agitated. Voices were starting to whisper in her head, and her core was beginning to burn in rage. Why was he such a nuisance?

'Don't you think the way she died was unnatural?'

'I said I don't know how she died. There was too much blood.' Her eyes met Mohite's. A flash of anger on her face made him put his cigar down and look at her gravely.

'What happened in the morning?'

'I told you everything!' She said in an exhausted voice, controlling her anger.

'Do you think a person could stab their own throat with such violence?'

'I can't say.'

'Even if they were committing suicide, they would hesitate at the last moment. The force would be blunted by the survival instinct coded in the genes.'

'I don't know.' Sama met his stare, trying not to be angry or scared.

'So, you think your mother chose this brutal method to kill herself and went through with it?' He asked again, the baritone deeper though his tone was still casual.

'I cannot say.'

'She's been handling knives for years, but you still think it could have been a freak accident?'

'That's what a freak accident is.'

'Just like Nik's accident, right?'

'I don't understand how he comes into this.' A vein in her forehead bulged when Nik's name fell on her unprepared ears. Mohite noticed.

'Was the railing cold when Sama jumped off?'

'What?'

'Answer me, or I will take it as a reason to lock you up tonight.' His eyes turned ice-cold, his voice adamant as iron. Sama clutched the edge of her chair.

'As I told you dozens of times before ... maybe, I don't remember, or rather, I was in no state to notice a trivial detail like that when she jumped.'

'Last time, you said you were positive that you were a metre away when she jumped. You are saying you didn't even notice whether the railing was cold?'

Her heart sank.

'I mean at some point I may have held it, but I don't remember the fucking temperature. Yes, I was a metre away when she jumped.'

'So your mother stabbed herself, or was it an accident?'

'She did try to reach her phone I heard some policemen saying. Couldn't it have been an accident?'

'Still doesn't explain the nature of the wound.'

'Then what do you think, sir?'

'I think she was stabbed.'

'How's that possible?' Sama began to weep again. 'I saw her in the kitchen alive and well when I left.'

'No one else did. Quite like in your sister's case.'

'I said hello to the neighbour when I left.' Her hands and feet had turned cold and sweaty. Whatever she did, however much she controlled, her heart had started to race. 'Everything was normal.'

'The neighbour wouldn't have seen or known that, though, even if things weren't normal. Her throat had been cut, and she couldn't have shouted for help.'

'Here I am, scared out of my wits because my mother died while I was happily driving to college, and you are trying to grill me about it?'

---

He fell silent and took another drag. *Maybe*, Sama thought, *he would stop now.*

'How can you say she died when you were driving to college?'

She stared at him, managing somehow to keep a straight face.

*Idiot, he's provoking you. Stop slipping.*

'The forensic team said it was in the morning at around that time.'

'Yeah?' He took another drag. 'Don't you think it's strange that it happened around the time you left?'

'Why should I think it strange? We were talking about Sama ... maybe her guilt was far more unbearable than I thought. Or maybe, as you said, it really was a freak accident. And that can happen anytime without warning, as in Nik's case, right?'

'That's a lot of maybes,' Mohite commented.

'This is painful for me. My sister died in front of my eyes, and today I saw my mother dead on the floor in my own house. Is there anything else you want to say?' she said in a frail, shaky voice. Mohite continued staring at her as he puffed on his cigar.

---

'I have a theory, but before I tell it to you, a few more questions. You said you lost your appetite and didn't eat. Why did you put your coffee mug in the microwave?'

'I thought I would drink it before leaving, but I didn't.' She frowned. Too many lies would get her caught. They would definitely look for fingerprints. If she said it was her mother who had put the coffee in the microwave, surely, they would verify the prints.

'That means you went into the kitchen before leaving.'

'Yeah, I hugged her before I left. I hugged her after a long time. Is that a crime?'

'We'll try to find your prints on her,' he said coolly. She froze, but managed to compose her features.

'My third theory is that she was made to stab her own throat somehow. The brute force with which the wound was inflicted suggests that to me. If it had been a suicide, I doubt she'd have dragged herself out of the kitchen. She tried to crawl out, however, and reach her phone. This suggests that she didn't want to die. I'd say that it might have been a freak accident if the table wasn't pulled away from her reach. The table was heavy, and the lines on the floor suggest that it was shifted recently. What do you think?'

Sama stared at him, feigning shock.

'Your third theory would be null and void if that table was recently shifted by myself or Mom, or by a servant cleaning the house.'

'Did you move it at any time?'

'Many times, not today, though.'

'Can you tell me the last time you moved it?'

'How can I remember such a trivial detail?'

'Well, your fingerprints were on the edge of the table. Better come clean now.'

'I don't understand where this is coming from, sir, but my prints would be all over the table. The couch next to it is my favourite place to sit in the whole house.' Her eyes filled with tears again. 'Mom would sit there with me for hours. We'd sit there chatting while I sampled the fruit salad she always made, and the pies and cakes ...'

He puffed on his cigar, his eyes still sharp. Her tears had no effect on him, she realized. It made the voices in her head louder and more irate.

'There's also something else that doesn't quite fit. Her writing "Sama" with her blood. This is not common in suicide cases. If it was guilt, she'd be too ashamed to display it, or she would mention it in a note or a message before committing suicide, not *while* she was dying. Also, writing Sama's name disproves the freak accident theory. No reason to write her dead daughter's name in her final moments, if that were the case. Surely, she'd try to use her remaining energy to reach her phone. Then again, even if it was someone else who stabbed her or made her stab her own throat, it still makes absolutely no sense.'

'So isn't your first theory—that of suicide—still the most plausible one? What reason other than guilt could have made my mother write her dead daughter's name?' Sama said.

'Well, that is a mystery!'

'Sorry, but as I see it, your third theory is spun out of the clouds.'

Mohite smirked. 'We'll keep your points in mind while investigating,' he said casually as he rose from his chair. 'I am really sorry for your loss. It is tough, I understand. Plus, you have to face an investigation now. I hope you are available whenever we need some answers, taxing as it may be.'

*He says it but doesn't mean it ... I can't slip.*

'I understand. Thanks for everything,' she said coldly, standing up with her arms crossed over her chest. There was no way she would shake hands with that man anymore.

---

The night seemed endless. Fear kept Sama awake. Inspector Mohite had come too close to the truth this time; his third theory was, in fact, the farthest from being spun out of clouds. She might have made a huge mistake that morning by letting her impulses take over, but she had been so angry that she couldn't help it.

On the road outside the house, Inspector Mohite paced up and down, the recorder in his pocket playing Sama's interview over and over again. He listened to every single word and tried to recall his own observations.

One thing stood out. Despite her apparent grief over losing her mother, she was able to counter each question logically. She didn't stutter or suffer from lapses of memory; her mind didn't shut down. Every statement she made was precise. Were they true? With her mood swinging erratically between sobs and angry glares, he could hardly tell.

Yet, something was off. He just couldn't identify the gap. Suddenly, a thought came to his mind.

'No, it can't be ... but then again, maybe ...?' he said to himself, puffing away at the third cigar of the night. Mohite watched a star twinkling between two black clouds. His hunch was getting stronger.

# PENITENCE

Her mother's funeral was two days later. Mrs Vyas's body had been handed over to the family after a lengthy post-mortem. No evidence of poison or other signs of wrongdoing could be deciphered. The nature of the stab wound, inflicted with such unusual strength, remained a mystery.

Her father had returned from the hospital before noon on the day of the funeral. He barely looked like himself anymore; his face was gaunt with grief. Sama sat with him and looked into his eyes as she tried to pacify him, like Sevita would have. He wasn't really listening.

At least, she thought to her satisfaction, he isn't as grief-stricken as he was at Sama's funeral. She had scored over her mother at last.

Some relatives had gathered at the house; there were rituals to be carried out. Kunal texted her that he wasn't being allowed to get out that day; his family was concerned and didn't want him to step out. Sama didn't like it one bit, but she replied that she understood his family's concerns. Friends and neighbours were horrified as the details of Mrs Vyas's death emerged. The lady who had ordered the fatal fruit salad was in a shambles.

'I had no clue. There was no sign of anything odd when I spoke to her! Not after Sama's death, nor the night before this happened,' she was telling Vikrant Singh after the funeral, who made extensive notes.

Sama had to shed tears and feign grief every second of the day. All the while, she was craving to get away on a date with Kunal.

*Mother was so useless. Even her death has caused nothing but trouble,* a voice said scathingly in her mind as she grit her teeth and kept up the pretence.

When everything was over and everyone had gone, after her father had taken pills to get some sleep, she finally went to her room. She sighed and sipped on her coffee, wondering what Kunal was doing and when she would see him again.

He had been texting her and had called her a few times, but they hadn't met for two days now. Something was gnawing at her insides, an uneasy fear. She felt the distance between them grow and it was unbearable. Should she start going to college? Should she ask him to see her?

Her phone rang all of a sudden. It was almost midnight. An unknown number flashed on her screen. Sama contemplated whether she should take the call or not. She decided to pick up. The caller broke the silence after a few seconds of heavy breathing.

---

'It's me.'

She remained silent.

'I know what you've done. Everything. This time, you can't throw me off.'

She stayed quiet.

'I have something on you. Something you wouldn't want people to know.'

'Don't call me again.'

She hung up and blocked the number. What could Andrew possibly know? Did Astha say something? Her heart raced, and her breathing became uneven. Acid pumped out of her heart, burning holes in her chest and gut. Her head began to split in half with a sharp pain. The voices were taking over.

'No ... no, stop!' She clutched her head. 'Why is that scum after me? Why is he doing this? I didn't share that video. I only threatened to ...' she muffled her screams.

The walls were starting to become distorted again. She squeezed her eyes shut, curling up on her bed.

It was no use. She needed to kill some moths and pin them on boards to let it all out. Her head was hurting so badly that she couldn't get up. All night she lay coiled on her bed, trying to make the voices go away.

When the morning dawned, she decided to go to college. She wouldn't be able to get through the day alone. She messaged Kunal and left on her scooty. On her way, as she crossed the bridge, she felt the chills course down her spine again. She stopped.

---

*How far did you stand from her? Was the railing cold?*

Sama looked at the blackish river below her. It was flowing quite forcefully, almost as violently as on that day. The clouds seemed to be gathering as if on a battleground. They thundered cold and loud.

Sama stepped closer and touched the railing.

*Cold. The railing is cold. How did he think of that?*

She thought, looking down at her moist hands. Raindrops dotted the railing. It wasn't as high as it should be; it wasn't safe. How did she miss all these details before? When she got back on her scooty, she also noticed the little room from which the man had seen them from afar.

*Someone did see us that day, but not clearly.*

She reached the college and parked her scooty. Kunal's car wasn't there yet. Sama walked towards the main building.

She could see the hill where she used to go during lunch breaks, where Nik had tried to scare her. If Kunal hadn't stopped her that day, there would have been four witnesses to a murder committed with a butter knife. Now that would have been some freak accident!

She passed the wall she used to hide behind to watch Sevita talk to Kunal. That's how she started falling for his bright smile. Would things be different if she hadn't watched them? It was useless to think about all that now.

Kunal came to the class not long afterwards.

'Sevita ...' He sighed and put his arms around her. People watched them. They all felt sorry for her. How terrible to lose your sister and then your mother in a span of months. Sama relished their sympathy. She relished his embrace much more.

*I wouldn't want things to be any different ... no way.*

She hugged him back, taking in the warmth of his body. She had what she wanted, and she needed to maintain it.

---

Classes ended early with warnings of an upcoming storm. Everyone went home before noon. Kunal let her take the scooty and park it outside her house, while he climbed in through her window.

'I'm so sorry I left that night. I was shaken,' he said and hugged her tight. 'When the policeman escorted me home, my family panicked. Didn't let me out of their sight.'

'It's okay; you are here now,' she said. She closed her eyes and listened to his heartbeat. A tingling sensation filled her with warmth. All her worries subsided. 'I missed you,' she said as she stayed in his arms. She felt warm and fuzzy. Her heart raced but not with fear.

She kissed his neck softly, working her way up to his lips. She squeezed his hands and pressed her body against his, feeling the rush of blood, the thrill.

'Sevita, not now.'

'What do you mean? I missed you so very much,' she said, breathing heavily and unbuttoning his shirt.

'This is not the right time. C'mon!' He held her arms, trying to stop her.

'Stop being a tease,' she said, her tone forceful. She got her arms out of his grip and pulled him towards her. Her nails were digging into his back.

'Sevita, I said no!' Kunal was aghast. He pushed her away, looking at her in shock. 'Your mother just died. You were so close to her … I can't believe this is you!'

---

Sama stared at him in disbelief. He had pushed her away. There was nothing more painful or humiliating than that. How could he do this?

'What does that have to do with my feelings for you? I love you,' she said, uncertainly.

She was unable to maintain her cool. Her face suddenly turned blank and cold. Kunal blinked, utterly perplexed. Just moments ago, she had seemed completely fine.

'There are other ways to be together and love each other,' he said, sounding alarmed. 'I love you, I want to stay with you, but this is not appropriate. It's not even been a week and you ... What's wrong with you?'

She was still looking at him coldly. What could she say that would not make him hate her? After all, she couldn't comprehend why it was inappropriate.

'You don't want to say anything?' Kunal asked her. Her cold stare made him uneasy.

'I'm not in the mood to spend time with you right now. Maybe I'll see you later,' she blurted and almost immediately regretted it. Kunal took a deep breath and tried to hold her, but she pulled away.

'I'm there for you, but I just don't feel like it right now. I understand it's difficult, Sevita, and you are not thinking straight,' he said gently. She stared at him emptily, without a word.

'Let's see each other tomorrow, okay? I'll pick you up,' he said and made his way out.

Sama stood like a block of ice for a long time after he left. Slowly, the icy anger started to melt and give way to a fierce rage. Hours passed as she stared at the distorting walls. They had formless mouths and eyes.

Her phone was ringing again, call after call from an unknown number.

'Yes?' She picked it up, knowing exactly who was on the other end of the line.

'Stop pretending you don't know me, Sevita!' Andrew shouted wrathfully. 'I saw you kill your mother. Your own mother!'

A sharp feeling split her head again. This time, it was not pain.

Something broke inside her.

'What do you mean you saw?'

'You know where I am. Come right away,' he said and hung up.

---

Kunal had driven to the edge of a hill, speeding as he drove away from Sama's house. He was agitated, alarmed and—he could hardly believe it himself—scared. The strength with which she had pushed him away had been surprising. Something that Astha had said had been gnawing at him ever since that day in the parking lot.

He lit a cigarette and took a drag. Thunderous clouds were whirling together in the distant sky. The wind had died down. He could hear the waves of the river as they glided one above the other. The afternoon had turned dark and grey.

It was weird to think that Mrs Vyas was capable of committing suicide because she felt guilty about Sama's death when she had never really loved her. He knew this because Sevita often worried about her mother's lack of affection towards Sama. It had been absent since childhood. Kunal himself had never seen Mrs Vyas talk to Sama or about her. She behaved as if Sevita was her only child. Why would she suddenly feel so guilty about her death? She had not even cried at Sama's funeral. Come to think of it, she had looked relieved.

Today, Sevita seemed relieved too. Yes, she seemed relieved, not sad ... as if a burden had been taken off her shoulders. Kunal started thinking about all the small things that he had chosen to ignore. Sevita had never been mean to Shruti in front of him, but he did notice the way Shruti looked at her. At first, he had put it down to Shruti's depression and her unrequited love. But now that he thought about it, he wondered if it could be something more. Also, he realized, he had never seen Sevita get so involved in Astha's life as she had in the last few days. She had always avoided going to Astha's place to avoid getting caught up in that family's affairs. She had always hated them for being cruel to Astha, especially her father. Why the sudden interest? Was it guilt about not being able to help Shruti?

'Astha,' he said and rubbed the middle of his forehead, 'what did she want to say to me?' He took his phone out and dialled her number, hoping that she would pick up. 'What?' he exclaimed. The number wasn't there. He didn't remember deleting her number. Then, he saw it. Her number was in the list of blocked numbers on his phone. He had never done that.

A sense of foreboding hit him. There was only one person who could have deleted and blocked a number from his phone without him suspecting anything. As he stared at his screen, flustered, he realized why Astha never called or messaged him after that day in the parking lot. As he was lost in these thoughts, an unknown number flashed on his screen.

'Hello?'

---

'Is this Kunal?'

The man on the other end of the line spoke in a rural dialect of Marathi. The mobile number also indicated that he was calling from outside Lavasa.

'Yes?'

'I found your number written behind a photograph, but decided to call you once things were ... settled here.' The man hesitated, sounding unsure and afraid. He gave Kunal an address and asked him to come as soon as he could.

The place was two hours away if he sped like a rocket. By the end of that conversation, his mind began to absorb a horrid realisation. His blood froze in his veins; he was on the verge of a panic attack. He tried desperately to calm himself and gritted his teeth.

Kunal reversed his car from the hilltop and sped towards the location the man had indicated. Black clouds were still gathering. The river coiled around the hills like a serpent in deep slumber.

It was the calm before the storm.

He reached the place in less than two hours, thanks to the deserted roads and his frantic driving. It was a small municipal hospital far away from Lavasa. He rushed inside and scanned the general ward section. His eyes fell on a petrifying sight at the end of the row. He crumpled to the floor.

---

Sama approached the door of the house in the woods and stopped midway. It was deathly quiet. The silence was broken by the sound of dead leaves and twigs being crunched underfoot. Someone was inside.

Sama's phone beeped. Another unknown number had sent her a video.

'Watch it.' Andrew's voice was loud and clear in the windless weather. Sama played the video. Her eyes widened in shock. Every moment of her mother's death flashed on her screen.

'You filthy prick, you placed a camera outside my house?' she said. Her jaws clenched.

'Five cameras. In different places and at different angles. All to catch you.' He sounded pleased. 'Just like you did to us.'

'Come on outside and face me.'

'Destroy everything you have on Astha.'

'You'll back off if I do?' she raged. She walked towards the house.

*That scum has the nerve to blackmail me! Make him pay* ... said the voice inside.

'That's the deal ...'

'So you, a pothead scoundrel, are striking a deal with me?'

'All I care about is Astha. So yes, I will keep my word,' he said loudly, still inside.

Sama entered the old house. It was dark and cold. The walls were cracked and peeling. The air was humid and heavy, and the smell of mould was overpowering. She saw him standing against a wall. His wild eyes made him look like a lunatic.

'Speaking of your bitch, I haven't posted anything online yet, have I? Why do you think I'll do it now?' Her face contorted, as if she became filthy just by looking at him.

'Because you are pure evil. Someone who can kill their own mother is the devil incarnate. You would do anything to anyone if you had the means and the opportunity.'

'Oh, you are the first person to understand me, Andrew.' Her lips curved into a crooked smile. Her shoulders relaxed as her palms warmed up. 'Fine, we can destroy the evidence we have on each other. Together, tonight. But remember, I don't miss much. I know how to check the original and how many copies were made. If you try to trick me, you die,' she said, the smile on her face never reaching her eyes.

Andrew was definitely intoxicated. He was looking at her groggily, his hands hidden behind his back. Sama knew he was holding more than just his phone.

'That's fair. I'll wait.'

'Cool, at midnight, then,' she said and turned to leave.

In one crazy leap, Andrew pounced on her. He screamed like a maniac as he tried to strangle her with one arm. He held a knife in his other hand. Sama was ready for him. She pushed him back with such force that he hit the ground with a thud. A small cry escaped his mouth. When his grip loosened, Sama escaped the snare of his arm and grabbed the knife from his other hand. She pinned him to the floor with her knees on his chest. A molten rage flowed through her body, but her mind was as clear as day. She swung the knife at his neck. Somehow, Andrew was able to grab her wrist, blocking the movement of her arm.

'You scum! DIE!' She screamed, pushing the knife further down with both her hands. For a while, he managed to keep her from stabbing him, sweating in fear, with his eyes fixed on the knife. Sama watched him put up a measly fight for his worthless life. The more she watched, the more disgusted she became. He did have some strength in his arms, but it wasn't enough to stop her.

Slowly, the knife inched towards his neck. He writhed under her, kicking his legs. Sama overpowered him, her knees clamping his ribcage. She pushed the knife down again with both her hands, making his arms buckle ever so slightly. The knife pierced his skin and the layer of flesh underneath.

'You chose the wrong person to mess with, and so did Astha. So did Shruti, so did Nik. Mom chose the wrong daughter to ignore. Sevita was just unfortunate ... that's all.'

---

Andrew's eyes widened with shock when she revealed the truth, but it was too late. He saw the cold, unfeeling face stare at him, as the knife reached his bone. Her head was tilted to one side. An astonishingly beautiful face could be so empty, and a frail-looking body could be so strong. He had miscalculated it all. The knife went through his neck like a pin in a moth's thorax. It sliced through to his spine. He was convulsing with pain. Blood splattered out of his mouth as he stared at her face and choked.

'We could have ended this without bloodshed, but you had to go and avenge that bitch. Now, it's time for penance,' she said as she pulled the knife out and wiped her hands on his shirt. 'So filthy ... ugh. I'm going to wrap you up in the sleeping bags you have here, cover you with the sheets and leave you on the mattress you used to fuck her on. You will rot here. No one will ever know.'

Sama's hands felt nice and warm. Her palms tingled with excitement. It was so satisfying to pierce a man's throat with one's hands.

In the next few hours, she had wrapped his body up and dragged him to a corner of the house. She took care not to leave any fingerprints and got rid of any evidence that might link her to the scene. She removed the camera she had installed in front of the house. It was easy to set the place on fire using Andrew's lighter, some dry leaves and firewood, and a bottle of kerosene she had found on the premises. She also made sure that a portion of the drugs he had on him was left unburnt, so that people would blame his drug problem if he was ever found. On her way out of the woods, she deleted her call history and the videos.

*The first thing I should do is remove his cameras,* she thought as she started her scooty.

# METAMORPHOSIS

Kunal couldn't believe his eyes. She was barely conscious and breathing slowly, painfully. Her head, arms and chest were bandaged. Slowly, she turned to look at him. The softness in those eyes was achingly familiar. Tears streamed down Kunal's face, and he sobbed, holding his head in his hands.

'Kunal,' she said weakly. Even in her condition, she was more concerned about him. The heart-shaped pendant he had given her dangled from her neck over her hospital gown. Sevita had lost a lot of weight. Her skin looked yellow, her eyes were sunken, and her body was ravaged. But she had survived.

'How did this happen?' His voice was choked with emotion, and more tears rolled down his face.

'I found her floating in the river. She seemed dead, but when I pulled her out of the water, I realized she wasn't. I had no choice but to bring her here to the hospital near my village and tell them she was a relative. If I told them I had found her floating in the river, there would be police. She needed immediate attention,' the old man who had called Kunal told him. 'Now that she's conscious and you are here, my duty is done.' Before Kunal could stop him, he left in a hurry.

Kunal remained on the floor, still crying.

'Didn't want the police to be involved ...' Kunal's cries turned into a sad laugh. 'Does he know what he let happen?'

'Kunal ... I gained consciousness only a few days ago. It's my fault too, because I hesitated ...'

'What?' He looked at her. 'You could have called me a few days ago? Why didn't you, Sevita? We could've saved your mother,' he cried.

'What ... what do you mean saved Mom?' She felt her heart jolt. Kunal was silent. His shoulders dropped, and his fists uncurled. How could he tell her that life, as she knew it, had changed forever?

'I've made a huge mistake, Sevita,' he said feebly through his tears. 'We need to go to the police. I'll call them now.'

---

'Inspector Mohite?' He wiped his face and tried to sound normal. The inspector had given his number to him while questioning him about Sama's alleged suicide.

'Yes?' Mohite's baritone was audible on the other end.

'This is Kunal. I want to talk about Sama ...'

'Go on?'

'This will sound insane, but Sama is alive, and she's in Lavasa right now. It was Sevita who fell, and I just found her in a hospital. Please believe me—'

'Prepare the vehicles. We're moving out!' Mohite shouted at his subordinates. 'Where are you? I hope you have Sevita?' Mohite asked.

'I'm with her right now,' Kunal said, surprised. 'Did you know this already?

'Good. I had a theory, but now I'll have evidence. Can you meet me near the Lavasa bridge? I can't risk anything else happening ...'

'I'll manage. We'll be there in two hours.' Kunal hung up and looked at Sevita. 'I know you are in no condition to move, but we have to go.'

'I'll come with you. I want to know what's going on.' Sevita was trying to get up. Kunal sprang up to support her, but before he touched her, he recoiled.

Sevita glanced at him with a sinking heart. Kunal's hesitation was a blow to her. A terrible possibility crossed her mind. Would their relationship ever be the same again? She managed to stand and get out of bed. Kunal had got a wheelchair for her. He took her to the car as quickly as possible. Soon they were on their way to Lavasa.

---

The sky thundered overhead as Sama rode towards her house. It was slowly turning dark, and a few drops of rain fell on her face.

Her house came into view. There were policemen in the front garden. She could see her father talking to them. Sama frowned. *What was going on?* Something told her to stay away. Her father looked completely confused, and the police seemed to be searching the property. Were they inside her room?

*What should I do? Should I come back later and find out?*

Sama felt a desperation about her. Things were spinning out of control. Would she lose Kunal? She didn't want to give him up. He was the reason for everything she had done!

The thought that she would never hold him in her arms again made the voices in her head shriek. There was no way out. It was time to leave this place, to disappear. She would come back and take her stuff later, when things were better. It started to rain. Sama sped her scooty towards the bridge. By the time she arrived she was completely soaked.

'Wait right there!' she heard a voice boom.

---

Sama's scooty came to a screeching halt. Three police vehicles blocked the road in front of her. It was raining, but she could see Mohite step out with a loudspeaker in one hand and a gun in the other. Other policemen followed the inspector. All of them had their guns out.

Then she noticed that Kunal's car was there too, parked at the entrance to the bridge.

*Kunal? Why?*

Sama frowned. Her confusion was replaced by dread when she saw a frail Sevita step out of Kunal's car. Her head was bandaged, her arm was in a cast, and she was walking with great difficulty. Her usually kind eyes reflected pain and sadness.

After everything she had done, Sevita was still here. And she was standing with Kunal.

*That scum had survived. Why? Why? Why? WHY?*

Her unfeeling eyes flickered with anger. Her hands curled into fists. Gadre was walking towards her with a gun and a pair of handcuffs. Sama turned her gaze on him. He looked uncertain for a second.

*Weak scum.*

She lunged and snatched the gun from him, kicking him

hard in the stomach with her knee. Gadre doubled up in pain. Sama grabbed him.

Mohite had not anticipated her move. He was shocked beyond belief. Sama had just overpowered a trained, experienced police officer, taking him hostage. She had the gun pointed at Mohite's head now and used Gadre as her shield.

'Sama, I–' Mohite tried to talk, but she refused to listen.

'No. You will all stay away from me,' she said loudly, retreating a few steps.

'You will never be able to run away. You know that. We will catch you.' Mohite was furious. 'Your secret is out in the open. We know you tried to kill Sevita, and that you were involved in the other deaths. I know you killed your own mother!'

Sevita gasped, her legs becoming weak.

---

'You have no proof.'

'I have enough to lock you up for years.'

The police personnel around him were more alert now. Sama watched them all for a second. She stopped walking backwards when she realized she was against the railing of the bridge. There was nowhere to go anymore. Police had sealed off the other end of the bridge; she had heard their cars screech to a halt in the distance.

It didn't matter ... she still had a hostage.

She glanced at Sevita and Kunal. So terrible was the shock of their mother's death that Sevita looked like she would pass out any second. Sama's gun moved slowly until it pointed straight at her sister. The police stopped their advance.

'Did you kill our mother, Sama?' Sevita cried, ignoring the gun pointed at her. Sama stared at her grief-stricken face, unable to feel anything. Her finger itched to press the trigger. She wanted those eyes to become lifeless, once and for all.

'Stop!' Kunal shouted and stepped in front of Sevita. Sama looked at him. His eyes—the eyes that would be enchanted by the mere sight of her—were dismayed and frightened. He was ready to stop her at the cost of his own life. Sama felt the familiar pin-pricks all over her body. She stared into his eyes. He stared back. They weren't the same anymore.

*He won't be the same anymore.*

Even if she killed Sevita then and there, it wouldn't change anything. She had lost everything. The rain had turned into a downpour. Thunderclaps shook the hills and lightning lit the violent river in lurid streaks. The storm was sweeping in over the land to thrash the bridge they stood on.

---

Sama's lips curved into a lopsided smile as she looked at him.

'It's no use now, is it, Kunal?' she said, but he couldn't hear her. Her voice had dropped to a whisper. The police were closing in from both sides. She watched Kunal look at her, burning his image into her mind.

Sama turned the gun towards the side of her head and pulled the trigger.

The sub-inspector fell on the road, and she swayed for a moment against the railing. Mohite ran towards her, but he was too late. Sama had fallen into the swelling river and disappeared. Sevita shrieked and finally blacked out. Kunal was frozen, staring at the spot where Sama had stood seconds ago.

The police swung into action. Sevita was rushed to the hospital. Kunal stood like a statue on the bridge despite the commotion around him. The image of her smile still haunted him.

'We need to leave. The weather department has asked us to evacuate the bridge,' a policeman told Kunal. He was barely in his senses, but he managed to get in his car and drive away from the bridge.

The police frantically looked around the bridge, fighting the wind and the rain. After a long fruitless search, they had to seal the area off and turn back. Mohite's fists were clenched, his brows creased. Slowly, every scene and every detail of the case flashed through his mind. A terrible tragedy had occurred in front of everyone's eyes, and no one had seen it coming.

'We'll never find the body. Not in this storm. And this time, there is absolutely no chance of survival ...' Vikrant told Mohite as he offered to light his cigar, taking shelter in a police car. Mohite took a long drag and exhaled.

'Maybe ...,' he said as they drove through the storm.

# EVOKED

The storm that had hit them was one of the worst in the history of Lavasa. Trees had been uprooted, buildings damaged and houses destroyed. It had lasted for a single hour—a long, dark hour. Even after it was over, an atmosphere of doom hung over the wooded hills and the river.

The next day, the whole town came to know about the events on the bridge. The news caused a sensation. There was no proof to connect Sama Vyas to the other deaths, but there were many speculations. Investigations were in full swing and search parties had been sent out to retrieve the body, this time beyond the river, in neighbouring towns.

Meanwhile, in one such neighbouring town, a young couple drove through the streets with R&B music at full volume. They had an old, beat-up SUV, but it ran like a cheetah on the road.

'What beautiful weather! Arun, should we speed up?' The young girl, wild and playful, thrust half her body out of the window. Her eyes were full of energy and life.

'No way, Jenny, we're at one-twenty already. Can't risk it on this slippery road! Plus, she might feel sick.'

The boy, tall and dusky, turned to look at the back seat. Amidst all their bags, volleyball equipment and gadgets sat a girl with wet hair. They had discovered her a few hours back, walking on the road with a small injury on the side of her head. Jenny had given her some dry clothes to change into and a cup of hot coffee from their thermos. She was still shivering with cold.

'Oh, you're right,' Jenny said. She turned to the girl. 'Should we turn the heater up? I can close the window for a while.'

'That would be good,' the girl said with a warm smile.

'Let's turn it up for Sevita, shall we?' She closed her window and smiled at Arun.

'Anything you say, ma'am!' Arun closed the windows and turned the heater up.

'It's really sad that you have nowhere to go now, Sevi,' Jenny said. She already had a nickname for the friendly girl they had given a lift to. 'It's terrible that your mother is no more and that you had to leave home because of the constant abuse. But don't worry. Such a life should be left behind. You're better off.'

'You're right,' the girl said, rubbing her shoulders.

'You know, we did the same.' She looked at Arun lovingly and squeezed his arm. 'I'm twenty, and he's twenty-two. We are adults, and we have the right to choose our own partners. Yet our families disagreed because I'm Christian and they wanted a Hindu bride for him. The world is so cruel to lovers.'

'So, we eloped. We are running away.' Arun grinned.

'That is certainly exciting. You're lucky to have each other,' Sevi said.

'Yes!' Jenny was excited. 'We're moving to Goa. I'm going to manage this beach shack, and he's going to work with a hotel group. I can manage my studies while we both earn. We'll be just fine, right, babe?'

'Of course! Life is going to be great. We will get married and live together.' He leaned over and gave Jenny a quick kiss.

'Sevi, come with us. We're starting on a new journey, and we need good friends,' Jenny chirped.

'I'd love to, if it is not a problem. I have nowhere to go, you know ...'

'Yayyy!' Jenny clapped. 'New life, here we come!'

They sped up and drove towards the Konkan coast. It would be a long journey by road. They would stop at many places on the way, enjoying the views of the beautiful monsoon-drenched landscape and making the most of every moment of their lives. Sevi smiled her brilliant smile. A bright flicker lit her eyes up from time to time.

*Let's leave the old life behind and begin a new one, away from that damned town and its people ... away from all the similar faces and names. Let's take a new name and live a new life,* said the voices in her head. They chuckled in Sevi's head, danced and celebrated as they watched the young girl in love, observing her expressions, body language and behaviour.

The happy young couple kept up a lively chatter, oblivious to the psychopath in the backseat. Sama leaned back to enjoy her ride into the open world, where she was free to do as the voices wished.

# ACKNOWLEDGEMENTS

> 'You can, you should, and if you're brave enough to start, you will.'
>
> – Stephen King, *On Writing: A Memoir of the Craft*

Even as one starts, a push is always helpful to keep the momentum going, especially for a writer. I am immensely grateful to Ravi Subramanian for giving my story a chance to be published in the *Shortz* series. Your support at every step has made this possible.

A big thanks to Vinita Nangia, the mind behind *The Times of India* Write India campaign, because of whom I met Ravi. It's a truly wonderful platform where aspiring authors can meet writers from all over the country. Being one of the top contestants of Write India was not only a boost to my confidence, but also the first step of my journey towards being a published author.

Sanghamitra, if a writer is the architect, then an editor is the builder. Thanks for your inputs, corrections, discussions and all the support for every element of this book. Gavin, thank you for your patience and for creating a cover that is exceptional. I'm also grateful to the team at Westland who worked relentlessly to make this book possible. What an exciting journey it has been!

Papa, thanks for being my inspiration for writing and for being my favourite storyteller. I write because you told me bedtime stories, because you printed out my first book when I was fourteen! You are not here to see me finally get published, but you knew I would get there, and every book I publish will be dedicated to you from my heart.

Last but not the least, to my family, friends, and especially my cousin Abhay who encouraged this procrastinating writer to complete my books and get them published. How could I have done this without you? I'm truly blessed to have you all in my life.

# ABOUT THE AUTHOR

**Ravi Subramanian** is the award-winning author of ten novels. His stories are set against the backdrop of the financial services industry. He has won the Economist Crossword Book Award three years in a row, as well as the Golden Quill Readers' Choice Award. His books have been translated into Hindi, Tamil and Latvian. Visit him at www.subramanianravi.com or connect with him on Twitter @subramanianravi or on Instagram @Ravisubramanian70.

**Mansi Babbar** is a content creator and has her own podcast, Horror Originals. She was one of the top ten contestants in the Times of India—Write India campaign. Next to writing stories, she loves to binge watch shows on Netflix, camp out on starry nights and eat good food! You can reach her on www.mansibabbar.com or on her Instagram account @mansi_19.

## 30 Years *of*

# HarperCollins *Publishers* India

At HarperCollins, we believe in telling the best stories and finding the widest possible readership for our books in every format possible. We started publishing 30 years ago; a great deal has changed since then, but what has remained constant is the passion with which our authors write their books, the love with which readers receive them, and the sheer joy and excitement that we as publishers feel in being a part of the publishing process.

Over the years, we've had the pleasure of publishing some of the finest writing from the subcontinent and around the world, and some of the biggest bestsellers in India's publishing history. Our books and authors have won a phenomenal range of awards, and we ourselves have been named Publisher of the Year the greatest number of times. But nothing has meant more to us than the fact that millions of people have read the books we published, and somewhere, a book of ours might have made a difference.

As we step into our fourth decade, we go back to that one word – a word which has been a driving force for us all these years.

Read.

Harper Collins · 4th · HARPER PERENNIAL · HARPER BUSINESS · HARPER BLACK · हार्पर हिन्दी

HarperCollins *Children's Books* · HARPER DESIGN · HARPER VANTAGE · Harper Sport